ROSE POINT

Karen marries Alan Denver and returns with him to the cliff-side house next to the lighthouse he tends. However, she knows nothing of the death — or even the existence — of his first wife. Then she begins to sense strange ghostly presences about the house, and her husband starts behaving oddly. She senses, too, that Alan's mother, who lives nearby, is trying to break up her marriage — but why? The truth lies hidden behind a locked door, and in a scrap of rose point lace . . .

V. J. BANIS

ROSE POINT

Complete and Unabridged

LINFORD
Leicester

First published in Great Britain in 1972

First Linford Edition
published 2015

A catalogue record for this book is available
from the British Library.

ISBN 978–1–4448–2302–8

Published by
F. A. Thorpe (Publishing)
Anstey, Leicestershire

Set by Words & Graphics Ltd.
Anstey, Leicestershire
Printed and bound in Great Britain by
T. J. International Ltd., Padstow, Cornwall

This book is printed on acid-free paper

1

It was called, I had been told, the graveyard of the Pacific. For centuries giant swells have pounded the sandstone promontory, and the roaring winds have twisted the few trees into grotesque parodies of their natural shapes. Here roam ghosts from the grim past, the souls of the seafaring men whose sailing came to an end on these jagged rocks. It is said that on a stormy night you might see their lanterns sparkling along the cliffs, like swarms of ghostly fireflies, seeking some final port.

We came to Point Dana by night, on a night when the waves of the ocean pounded and the winds roared across the land, hurling sheets of water at the windshield of the car so that we crept the last few miles along that narrow, rough road that led up to the house.

This is how they must have felt, I thought, those sailors of old in their little ships, buffeted by wind and water, trying to find their way in the darkness, eyes scanning the distance for a flash of light.

I saw a flash of light, a mere wink of it ahead. It went and came again, and I remembered uneasily those stories I had heard of the ghosts that wandered here.

I put my hand on Alan's leg and said, 'Look.'

He patted my hand without turning his head, as if he guessed the line my thoughts had been following. 'Almost there. That'll be mother, out with a lantern to guide us. She must have been watching and saw the headlights. You should hear the foghorn soon.'

I looked all around, seeing nothing but darkness. 'I don't see the lighthouse,' I said.

'You can't see it from here. It's down below us, on a rock beneath the high cliffs. But it can be seen from the ocean.'

I did hear the foghorn then, piercing the night with its mournful cry.

The road turned, becoming a drive. The rain seemed to lessen in the beam of our headlights now that we were no longer driving against it. I saw the house, bigger and more lavish than I had expected, not the sort of California-style house I was accustomed to. Indeed, it looked more European than American. Scandinavian?

Made of stone, it looked not unlike a miniature castle, although rather a simple one. The central structure was flanked by two wings that formed a small courtyard into which we drove now. Turrets rose into view on either side where the wings joined the main building, and I wondered if they looked out upon the sea. They must afford spectacular views.

The courtyard was walled. That explained why I hadn't seen the lights of the house as we approached, although now that we were within the courtyard I could see that the house was brightly lit. That other, flickering light I had seen had become a rain-cloaked figure holding a lantern, moving into the courtyard as we drove up, hurrying about the car now to the driver's side.

'Alan, welcome home,' a woman's voice greeted him as he opened his door. She saw me then, and asked, 'Why, who's this?'

'Let's get inside first, okay?' Alan said, laughing. 'Before I drown.'

There was a scramble to get our coats about us, and a dash across the courtyard in the pouring rain to the open front door. It let us into a wide hall with a high, arching ceiling and a red tile floor. Straight ahead stairs led up to another level. Beyond the stairs and through an arch I could see doors, one of them open upon what was apparently the kitchen. The living room was to our right, through another open arch. A fire burned in the fireplace there, bright and warm, dispelling any ghosts that might have tried to follow us inside. It was a lovely home; no doubt the more so to my eyes because of the storm through which we had been driving.

I had merely put my coat over my head and wrapped it about me when I got out of the car. Now I slid the coat off, giving my long hair a shake, and laughed, partly with relief that we were here after a long and arduous drive, and partly with delight because the house was so unexpectedly lovely and I was so very happy.

'Mother,' Alan said, putting an arm about my waist and pulling me close. 'This is Karen.'

She had removed her rain cloak with its all-concealing hood, holding it at arm's length while it ran water on the red tiles. She was a handsome woman. Probably she had once been beautiful, but she had lived too long in the salt air and the harsh winds. She looked like an old sailor herself, but fast and light with her movements, and with an inquisitive way of cocking her head to one side, looking from one of us to the other, and back.

'Karen . . . ?' she repeated.

'Karen Denver,' he said, grinning from ear to ear. For a moment she did not comprehend the use of his — of their — last name. 'My wife. We were married this morning.'

('We'll surprise her,' he had said to me. 'She'll be delighted.')

He had been half right. She was indeed surprised, but by no means delighted. Her hand went to her face as though she

5

had been struck. I seemed to hear my father's voice at my ear, saying, as he so often had, 'Karen, someday you'll learn to look before you leap.'

'I . . . I don't understand,' she stammered, still quite dumbfounded by his announcement.

I freed myself from his embrace and came toward her, feeling all at once guilty for our thoughtlessness. 'We should have called you.' I gave her an apologetic smile. 'It was all so quick. I'm afraid I just didn't think far enough ahead.'

'We wanted to surprise you,' Alan added.

She made a valiant effort to regain her poise. 'Yes,' she said, 'you said on the phone that you had met a girl . . . ' She let the sentence linger unfinished, however, and said to me, 'Well, welcome, of course, Miss . . . '

'Karen,' Alan said. 'And not Miss.'

'Karen,' she said. 'Forgive me. I was a little taken aback.' She did manage a smile then, albeit a rather wan one.

'You had every right to be,' I said. 'I think it is we who should ask you to

6

forgive us. We were rather selfish, I'm afraid.'

'It's quite all right.' She put her coat on the rack in the hall, quickly regaining her composure. 'My son has always been an impulsive person. But come; let's not stand out here in the hall. We have a fire going and I've kept some food warm in the kitchen. It'll just take a minute to put it on the table. Alan, why don't you get out of those things and get into some dry clothes.'

'They'll be all right,' he said. 'I'll just sit in front of the fire for a while.'

'Nonsense,' she said in a commanding tone. 'Those things are soaked. You go on now and change. Karen will help me set up.'

She did not seem to think I might be a little damp too, but it was a forgivable oversight. She was used to fussing over Alan. I was a new factor to which she hadn't yet adjusted her thinking.

I had seen, though, that Alan bristled a little at her tone of voice. I felt that this was not a new contest between them. She seemed in the habit of asserting her authority and Alan gave an impression of liking his independence. I suspected they had clashed on this point before.

This time, at least, it was Alan who gave in with a good-natured laugh. 'She still thinks I'm in diapers,' he said to me. 'I warn you, she'll probably want to boss you around too.'

'You need someone to tell you what to do,' she said.

I went with her to the kitchen and Alan went up the stairs in the hall, taking them two at a time. In a surprisingly short time everything was ready. After several hours of driving through rain and darkness, it was good to sit down to the hot supper she had kept for us.

'It's only chowder,' Mrs. Denver said, ladling the richly scented stew into bowls. She had put herself to making us comfortable and the strained atmosphere that had greeted our arrival had relaxed somewhat.

'It smells wonderful,' I said, and, a moment later, 'and tastes even better.'

I wasn't merely being polite. The chowder tasted fresh and of the sea and warmed us through, driving out any lingering chill. We ate huge slabs of bread with it, baked no more than an hour or two earlier, and followed it with a cherry cobbler warm from the oven.

I sensed Mrs. Denver was a woman like my own mother in some ways, who derived her greatest pleasure from satisfying the needs and appetites of her husband and family. With her husband gone, and only Alan to fuss over, I suspected this sort of lavish treatment was more the rule than the exception.

She had regained her presence of mind, and applied herself to being friendly and charming, with success. She was intelligent and polite, and the evening moved along pleasantly enough.

Yet for all Alan's pleasure in being with me, for all the loveliness of my new home, and for all Mrs. Denver's charm, now directed to me, I felt an underlying air of tension. She did not like me. No, perhaps that was not quite it. It was more that she did not like my being here. I don't think that I, as an individual, mattered that much. She would have resented anyone in my place, I suspected.

I chided myself that I was being impatient. It was not so very unusual that a mother should be a little possessive of her only child and just a trifle jealous of his new wife. I knew couples enough who had experienced this sort of difficulty, and particularly was this true where the mother was a widow.

And living the isolated life she lived could not but increase this likelihood a hundredfold. Moreover, we had given her no opportunity to prepare herself for the fact of our marriage, but had presented her instead with a fait accompli.

It was for me to take the initiative in establishing the friendship that I wanted with her. I made a promise to myself to take no offense at her air of aloofness and to make every effort to become real friends.

I did not forget that I too was embarking on what Alan had warned me was a very lonely way of life. Aside from the two of them and the other man who worked the Point Dana lighthouse with Alan, my nearest neighbors were ten miles away. The nearest town was one called Lompoc, some thirty-five miles distant. I would need Mrs. Denver's friendship if I was to be spared the ordeal of loneliness.

'You look like you're deep in thought,' Alan said to me.

I smiled across the table at him. Was it possible that a month ago I had not even known him? In such a short period of time I had come to know every feature of that handsome face, to love the way the dark hair tumbled across the forehead, to look for the almost invisible dimple when he smiled very broadly. My heart sang with the fullness of my love for him.

'I was thinking how pleasant it is here,' I said, flashing a smile back at him that added all the rest that I was thinking. He saw it, and understood, and we pledged our love once again, silently, in a single glance.

'I hope you will still think so after a few weeks of our isolation,' Mrs. Denver said, bringing us back to earth.

'Make that a few years,' Alan said.

'Alan says you have no family,' Mrs.

Denver said, letting the other subject lie.

'That's right. I lost my parents and my brother a few months ago, in an accident.'

'I'm sorry. It must have been a very sad experience for you.'

The old grief knocked at the door of my consciousness, but I held the door stubbornly closed. That was the past. I had been given an opportunity for new happiness. It was in this I should live — this moment, this happiness.

'We were a very close family,' I replied matter-of-factly. 'It left me quite alone, until Alan came along and found me.'

I am not awfully good at explanations, or at telling people how I truly feel about things, especially about things that matter greatly. I hoped this last remark would make it easier for her to understand the suddenness of our marriage, and how I could have come, with so little hesitation, to this isolated point.

Alan had offered me an opportunity to be alone, with him, without being lonely. He too had been lonely, and had welcomed the possibility of bringing me here with him.

Of course, to explain that clearly in words, I would have to explain all that we felt for one another, and how did one explain love so that it made any sense? On an impulse, I leaned across the table to put my hand over hers.

'I do want us to be good friends,' I said fervently, and meant it.

'I'm sure we shall be.' She smiled but her smile was only a showing of teeth.

Be patient, I told myself, and gave her hand a squeeze.

When we had finished eating, she and I cleared the table while Alan returned to the living room. She would have washed the dishes as well, but I protested with such vigor that she yielded and left them for me to do.

'After all, I don't want you to be made into a housekeeper for us,' I said laughing.

'I've kept house for Alan for years,' she said. 'I've never minded.'

A note of sadness had crept back into her voice. I sought in my mind for something I could say that would bring her closer to me.

'I'll probably have to rely on you a great deal as it is,' I said. 'There's so much I don't know about keeping a house. You can teach me.'

'I'll try.' We had come into the hall from the big, old-fashioned kitchen. 'Well, I suppose I should be going home.'

Alan, hearing us, stepped into the hall. I saw that he was a different man now from the one I had met and married. He had changed subtly, as everyone does, now that he was at home, in his own familiar surroundings. There was much I did not know about my husband. I hoped his mother would help me there too.

'Oh,' I said, remembering the weather, 'but it's still storming. We'll drive you home, won't we, Alan?'

She put on her voluminous rain cloak. 'Nonsense.' She gave me a shake of her head. 'I know every rock along these cliffs, and every gust of wind. I assure you I can be home much faster walking than you could get me there in the car.'

'She's right,' Alan said, reassuring me.

'If you live here as long as I have — almost forty years, now that I think of it — you'll learn not to be intimidated by a little rain, my dear.'

I felt a twinge of annoyance that she had said 'if and not 'when' and at once scolded myself for being so quick to take offense.

'I don't know,' I said doubtfully. She had opened the door and the storm outside was still considerably more than a little rain, to my way of thinking. A cold wind swept through the hall.

'It's no use arguing with her,' Alan said with a laugh. 'We've been through this sort of thing before and in the end she always does exactly as she pleases.'

'And I expect everybody else to do as I please too,' she said. 'That's what he's always telling me, at any rate.'

I thought perhaps he was right, but I said nothing.

She gave Alan a kiss on the cheek and came to me to do the same. 'My husband always said I was harder than any of the rocks out there on the cliffs. I didn't used to think so, but in time I learned he was right. You have to be hard to live here.'

'I hope I'm hard enough,' I said.

'We shall see,' she said. 'Time alone will tell.' Her expression, the quick look of doubt that flashed over her countenance, said all too clearly that she did not think I was. There would be no passive acceptance from her quarter. I would have to prove myself to her.

We stood at the door, watching as she went across the courtyard with her lantern, leaning against the wind. In the distance, the foghorn repeated its basso-profundo call. I had wondered if it would prove an annoyance, that regular, insistent sound. In truth, however, its very regularity made it eventually inconspicuous. I had already grown accustomed to it, and did not notice it without consciously directing my attention to it. It blended with the scene and became a part of the view and the night and the storm.

At the gate Alan's mother paused to wave to us. We waved back and then she disappeared into the stormy night.

I had a sudden feeling, I did not quite know what or from where it came. It might have been fear, except that I had nothing to be afraid of. It was as if, in the old saying, someone had walked across my grave. I shivered involuntarily.

'You're right,' Alan said, his arm about my waist, 'it's cold out here.'

I looked up into his face, that wonderful, finely chiseled face, and all of my fears and doubts vanished, just as the storm vanished beyond the closed door. What had I to fear when I was here, with my beloved?

⋆   ⋆   ⋆

Our bedroom was beautiful, with a fine old bed and a huge Spanish chest. The windows looked out upon the ocean and from them, for the first time, I saw the lighthouse, with its ever burning light. It stood atop a jagged rock a hundred feet or more above the ocean, its beam parting the darkness like a knife. It looked certain and unchanging, and I thought of what a comfort it must have been to so many men, with its piercing light and warning foghorn.

'It's beautiful,' I said when Alan came

17

to stand behind me, putting his arms about me.

He laughed. 'My mother's right. You may feel differently after a while. He gets on your nerves sometimes.'

'He?'

'The lighthouse. We call it a he.'

I looked at the light again. 'Yes, it does seem to have a life of its own,' I said. 'He looks like a watchful sentry, I think.'

'I would have said an accusing judge,' he said. 'Stern and unforgiving.'

I was surprised by that and looked up into his face. He did not look amused, but quite sober.

'And what does he accuse you of?' I asked, trying to tease a smile out of him.

I did not get my smile, however. He let go of me and turned away. 'It's late,' he said and disappeared into the bathroom.

I looked out at the lighthouse again, wondering if in time I too would see it — him — as stern or threatening. Now, of course, I was seeing everything through a haze of romantic enchantment, but I was sensible enough to know that in time that would lessen.

I was still at the window when Alan came back into the bedroom. I started to turn around, and paused.

'Oh,' I said, 'there's someone out there. On the rocks.'

He came to stand beside me. I pointed to the spot where I had seen someone, or something, move. It had been quick, the flitting of a shadow. The beam from the lighthouse thrust out over the water. Between that and the distorted rectangle of light from our window, there was darkness and rain.

'I don't see a thing,' Alan said. He put a hand on my waist. 'Come to bed.'

I peered intently out into the night. 'But I did see someone,' I said stubbornly. 'I'm sure I did.'

'There's nobody around,' he said, 'Except Farroday. He's my relief, but he isn't likely to be out climbing around on the rocks at this hour of the night. Or anyone else, unless you think my mother's hanging around for a breath of salt air.'

He was teasing me, grinning broadly. His somber mood of a few moments ago had disappeared and, confronted with his open good nature, my mood lifted too.

'I suppose you're right.' I turned away from the glass. He kissed me warmly and I forgot about shadows flitting across the rocky seascape.

'Maybe you saw one of the ghosts,' he whispered a moment later.

I laughed, but once again I had an unaccountable sense of uneasiness, as if it were a premonition of things to come. I was glad for more than one reason that I was in my husband's arms.

★   ★   ★

I woke to golden streams of sunshine pouring through the windows and across our bed. I lay for a moment and watched the motes of dust dance in the light.

When I turned my head, I saw Alan was already awake and watching me. He gave me a sleepy smile and a good morning kiss. In the distance I could hear, faintly, like the murmuring of an impatient audience in a theater, the waves on the rocks.

'I hope you slept well, despite the

ghosts,' Alan said.

'Beautifully. You tossed and turned, though.' I had already learned that my husband was a fitful sleeper. 'Something seemed to be bothering you.'

He shrugged it off as of no consequence. 'Probably the tension of the long drive last night,' he said.

'What were you dreaming, anyway? You kept mumbling.'

'What did I say?' He looked more amused than concerned. He ran a finger fondly through my hair, fanning it across the pillow.

'I couldn't make out a word,' I said, laughing. 'I listened carefully, too. I thought maybe I'd hear some other woman's name.'

'Wake me up next time and I'll listen too. I might learn something.' He kissed me. 'I never remember my dreams.'

Sometime later, I asked, 'How did you get the scar?'

'Do I have one?' He seemed surprised.

I propped myself up on one elbow. 'You can't not know it's there.' A jagged line ran a good three inches from his forehead down to his left temple. Sometimes his hair, inclined to be unruly, fell across it, more or less concealing it, but he could hardly have looked at himself much in the mirror without knowing the scar was there. I had seen it the first time I had looked at him up close.

He did, after all, know of its existence, because he put a hand up to it without hesitation, tracing the line with one finger.

'This? I don't remember where it came from.'

'It came from an awfully nasty cut.' I reached up myself to touch it. 'It hardly seems the sort of thing one would forget so easily.'

He caught my hand in his and brought his face down toward mine. 'Am I so ugly then, with my scarred countenance?'

The breath caught in my throat as I realized all over again how much I loved him. 'No,' I whispered, bringing my arms up about his neck, 'not ugly.'

Later, we went down to breakfast in a little nook in the kitchen, from which we could watch the waves on the rocks. With the exception of the wings off the main structure, all of the rooms looked out over the ocean. The architect had designed it to take maximum advantage of the breathtaking view.

'It seems elaborate for a lighthouse keeper and his wife,' I said of the house.

'It wasn't built for one. The man who designed it and built it was rather wealthy. The import trade in San Francisco, as I understand it. This was his retreat. The lighthouse came later. Someone just counted the wrecks that had taken place and stuck it here, with a little cottage.'

'Where Farroday lives?' He'd told me this on the drive up.

'Yes. And later, when the original builder died, this place became something of a white elephant. Nobody wanted a house this big and this elaborate, stuck out here in the middle of nowhere. It passed through several hands. The last owner died intestate and the house became the property of the state. It was a great deal simpler for the Coast Guard to take it over as a second house for the keepers and their families than it was to tear it down and build the new one they had decided they needed.'

'I'm surprised your mother didn't stay on here. There's so much room. It must have been awfully lonely rattling around here by yourself.'

'A little. My father was the keeper here before me. When he retired, they built their place up the coast. He wanted to be by the ocean that he knew and loved, but he didn't want to look out every morning and see the lighthouse.'

I knew from our earlier conversations that his father had been dead five years. Alan had been twenty-one at the time and already in charge of the lighthouse. I wondered briefly that his widowed mother had not moved back to this house then, but recalling the woman I had met last night, I thought she might prefer her independence. She was not a woman likely to be bothered by loneliness, and perhaps she too did not want to wake in the morning and see the lighthouse that had dominated the landscape of her life for so long.

It was time finally to go out and see

firsthand the vistas I had so far only seen at a distance.

'Farroday's been running things on his own since I've been gone,' Alan explained as we went out. 'I expect he'll be glad to have me take over for a while.'

We followed a path that led us to and along the cliff, to a spot where rough-hewn wooden steps with a crude railing made a dizzying descent down toward the rock on which stood the lighthouse. I instinctively held back for a moment, intimidated by that descent virtually into the pounding surf itself.

Alan took my arm. He must have sensed my moment of hesitation, but he did not comment on it. Instead, he began to talk of the history of the Point.

'The Point's had a history of tragedy ever since Cabrillo, the first of the Spanish explorers, sailed north up the Santa Barbara Channel in fifteen forty-two. He rounded the point, but was forced to turn back because of a heavy storm. He reached San Miguel Island, but he was injured there, and died.'

He paused in our descent of the steps

to point to the rocky beach below. 'During the nineteenth century,' he said, 'the beach there and the offshore reefs were littered with whalers and three-masted schooners. The whole swell of the Pacific Ocean rolls in here before a southeaster, and it breaks so heavy a surf in the shallow waters that it's dangerous for any ship to lie near the shore.

'At that point there,' he went on, pointing in yet another direction, 'the greatest peacetime disaster in the Navy's history took place, September eighth, nineteen twenty-three. Seven U.S. destroyers played follow the leader and dashed themselves to pieces against the coastline. There were five hundred men aboard the ships. Twenty three of them were lost. The others were brought ashore by use of raft and buoy. Some of them came floating by on a raft and a watch-keeper heard them shouting. They were hauled up the steep rocks in the dark with only the light of a hand-held lantern.'

'What about the light in the lighthouse?' I asked. 'Wasn't it burning to warn the ships?'

He nodded. 'Yes, but it just didn't pierce the fog, and the wind carried the noise of the foghorn inland. For years afterward you could see steel fragments rusting in the surf.'

We continued down. The base, by the lighthouse, had looked from above to be virtually on the water, but in fact it was one hundred feet or so above sea level. Winds whipped us as we walked to the lighthouse itself. The building looked like a little sea cottage atop which had been mounted a short tower that housed the light.

'The lighthouse itself was established in eighteen fifty-six,' Alan explained. 'The incandescent oil vapor lamp was replaced in nineteen forty-eight by electricity, but the lens is the original cut glass prism.'

A brass plate attached to the base read: 'Revolving Light Fresnel System, constructed by the order of the Honorable Secretary of the Treasury and of the Lighthouse Board. Henry Lepaute, Constructor, 1856.'

To my surprise the top of the tower, where the light was housed, was open, walled by iron bars and rails, but unprotected from the wind and rain. One entered below through a heavy wooden door, standing open just now, and climbed twisting, dark stairs, to suddenly emerge into the open air. I found myself thinking how it must be like here in a storm, with wind and water whipping across this unprotected area.

The view was spectacular, though. One could see for miles along the coast and, of course, the ocean stretched without break to the horizon.

I heard a sound on the stairs and a moment later a stranger appeared at the top, coming into the open room, a big bear of a man with a reddish moustache and slightly shaggy hair. He looked amiable. I thought from what Alan had told me that he was probably the other man who lived and worked here.

Alan put an arm about me. 'Hi,' he said. 'Karen, this is Jim Farroday, the other keeper here. Jim, this is my wife, Karen.'

He looked at us with unabashed surprise. 'Well, I'll be a monkey's uncle,' he said, but the next moment he was pumping Alan's hand enthusiastically.

'Congratulations, you devil you, you might have warned me.'

'I didn't know myself until the last minute,' Alan said, laughing.

Jim turned a smile of genuine welcome on me and I sensed that he would be a friend if I needed one.

'Welcome to the Point,' he said, taking my hand more decorously. 'And I wish you the best of luck.' He winked and added, 'You'll need it with him.'

I smiled and said, 'Thank you.'

'How'd things go?' Alan asked him when the pleasantries had been exchanged.

He remarked about one or two apparently minor incidents that had occurred and made mention of the fact that one of the buildings was in need of repainting. 'With the wind and the salt air, a paint job doesn't last too long here,' he said to me in the way of an aside.

I felt there were probably a number of things they would want to go over together, and said, 'Why don't you two excuse me? I can find my way back all right.'

29

Outside, I paused once again at the landing by the steps, looking out over the ocean. So many lives had been lost here, so many men vanquished in man's seemingly endless battle with the ocean. And still the waves licked at the rocks as if trying to reach me, as if hungry for yet another life.

I shuddered. That was hardly the train of thought for a new bride to be following. I turned and began to climb the steps, telling myself that the ocean, like most of nature, could be man's friend or his foe, depending upon the man.

And wasn't it the same with human nature? Look how quickly Jim Farroday had offered me his friendship.

I looked up and saw Mrs. Denver at the top of the steps, not coming down, but seemingly waiting for me to ascend. She smiled, but it was not the genuine smile of willing friendship that Farroday had given me. There was something wary in her look. Here was no offer of friendship, but a careful weighing of what she saw.

All in all, I didn't think I fared well in that scrutiny.

2

We went in, Mrs. Denver and I. She had brought some freshly baked croissants in a little basket.

'I do a lot of baking,' she said, putting them in their basket on the kitchen table. 'One has time here for the domestic niceties. There are few distractions.'

I put on a fresh pot of coffee and when it was done we had it with the rolls. They were still warm and quite delicious.

'You'll have to teach me to make them,' I said, helping myself to a third. 'I'm afraid Alan is going to find eating a disappointing experience after your cooking.'

'You don't cook well?' she asked, cocking an eyebrow. I had the impression she hoped the answer would be negative.

'Not this well,' I answered. 'I manage well if I keep it simple, but I'm sure there's so much I could learn from you.'

'I suspect you're being modest,' she

said. Once again she seemed to reject my tentative efforts at friendship. Her gaze drifted away from me, not purposefully, but rather as if there were simply nothing in my direction to anchor it there. I felt oddly insubstantial as a result, as if I were no more than one of the ghosts that were said to haunt these cliffs. She had dismissed me, like one of them, as something to be ignored.

When she did look at me there was a sensation that she was instead looking at whatever was beyond me, looking through me, as it were. It was an unnerving habit, the more so because it did not seem as if she were doing it consciously or deliberately to upset me, but rather because that was simply the way it was.

She stayed for lunch. I was actually a little surprised that she accepted without quarrel my insistence that she sit and let me prepare the meal. I half expected her to make an issue of it, but she seemed content to keep up a polite flow of conversation while I worked.

Lunch was rather easy. There was some of last night's chowder, to be reheated. I looked through the stores in the cupboard and opened a few cans.

When Alan had joined us and was sitting down at the table, she said, 'Alan likes coffee with his lunch.' She gave him a sweet smile.

'It's made,' I said, getting up to fetch the pot. 'I was going to pour it after we'd eaten.'

Seated again, I passed Alan one of the serving dishes. 'Alan doesn't like green beans,' his mother informed me.

I nearly mentioned that she had watched me preparing them without offering any comment at the time. I felt a bit piqued. I could not help thinking that I seemed less capable of making Alan comfortable than she did.

Don't be silly, I told myself, she's had years in which to learn everything about him — his likes and dislikes, his moods, his inclinations. In time I would know them all too. Still, it rankled just a little, and I suppose my annoyance must have shown.

'Maybe I'll try some anyway,' Alan said, taking the dish from me.

'You never liked them before,' his mother said.

'Doesn't do for a man to get into ruts,' he replied, and helped himself generously.

I gave my mother-in-law a friendly smile.

When Alan had finished his lunch and gone back to work, his mother offered to clean up the kitchen.

'No, I'll manage it,' I told her. 'I've little enough to do here as it is. I suppose time will hang a little heavy on my hands.'

She dismissed that with a shrug. 'Then I suppose I'll be on my way,' she said. 'I don't want you to think of me as underfoot. It's my natural inclination to want to boss people around, Alan especially. I will try to stay out of your hair, though.'

Her smile when she said this was so sincere that I felt a little guilty for some of the things I had been thinking. I said, perhaps too eagerly, 'Oh, no, I want you to come over often, even if it's only to boss us around. I'll need the company if I'm not going to get awfully lonely. I have the entire day to myself here.'

'We're never completely alone,' she said. 'You do understand that, don't you?'

'Yes, of course,' I said. I had been raised in a home that was quietly religious. I assumed she made reference to our maker, and I shared her opinion that he remained with us, but I did not, as a rule, discuss my religious beliefs with others, considering it a personal matter.

To my surprise, however, she added, 'They are with us.'

'They?'

She smiled and said, 'You'll understand, in time.'

With that, she was gone. She went out the kitchen door and I stood watching her follow the path to the cliff. She did not turn towards her own house, but went instead to the steps leading down to the lighthouse.

I went to the kitchen window and from there I could see her descend to the landing. I watched her until she disappeared inside of the lighthouse, but I had a feeling of guilt then, as if I were eavesdropping on a private conversation. It was a silly thought, since short of yelling, a human voice could hardly have carried that distance. Nonetheless, I turned from the window and helped myself to the last of the coffee.

Alan's mother seemed to be making an effort to be pleasant and thoughtful. I had to remind myself that she was unaccustomed to company and to the sometimes touch and go process of establishing friendships. That process, I thought, was like a muscle that got stronger as one used it, but that could atrophy with disuse. I must give her time to regain the use of it.

Time. That was the key here. That was the thing most lacking in the relationship between Alan and myself. We had met and fallen so quickly in love and there had not been time enough to get really acquainted. I had trusted to instinct.

What we shared now was the flame of love, however, and I knew that the fire from which it blazed must be carefully banked if it was to burn a long time and not burn itself out quickly. For this I needed time and a wisdom I could only pray I would find within myself.

Time would help me too, I felt certain,

in winning the friendship of Alan's mother. I must accept for now the fact of her reserve and her resentment of me. In time, if I were patient and persistent in my efforts, I would surely overcome these.

I put these thoughts aside for the present, and turned my attention instead to my work. I had only half unpacked the night before, and now I went upstairs to finish that job. When I had packed our cases, I had done so rather hurriedly, and in a nervous state, as befitted a new bride. I was not too surprised, as a result, to find some of the things a little mussed. The afternoon passed quickly while I ironed.

It was not until the following morning, when Alan had gone out to work, that my thoughts turned again to Mrs. Denver's parting remark.

'*They are with us,*' she had said. I frowned as I looked out the kitchen window, toward the ocean. Had she meant these, the waves and the rocks that I could see from here? They were indeed with us, almost as if a living presence hovering on the edge of our awareness.

Or had she meant the ghosts who were

supposed to linger here? She made light of them, but at the same time she had not said she did not believe in them. Were they real to her, haunting her? Did the shades of lost men attend her, perhaps assuaging a little the heavy burden of her loneliness?

Something stirred uneasily within me, some childish and since forgotten fear of the dark, of things that moved about us not quite seen, of outlines dimly perceived. I could feel as primitive man had felt as he huddled near his fire, stirring uneasily at the sounds in the shadows beyond its glow, and I thought how long was the memory of man.

Something did indeed stir then, something quite real and quite noisy. A door banged open in the front of the house, sending me a foot or so off the floor. I chided myself for my foolish train of thought, and went into the hall in time to see a plump cloud of a woman scudding down the hall before the wind from the open door. Her hair was white, her dress and her complexion were pink, and her eyes were as clear and blue as the sky.

She saw me and stopped abruptly, as surprised as I was to see her, but this was a cloud born to sail and to envelop in softness, not a wisp to drift and spend itself.

'Hello,' she said, without a trace of shyness, 'who are you?'

I laughed and said, 'I was about to ask you the same thing. I'm Mrs. Denver.' I saw her quick frown of puzzlement, and added, 'Alan's wife.'

She slapped a hand to her cheek with such violence that it seemed to jar her mouth open. 'Well, land's sake,' she said, and with scarcely a pause, she rushed to take my hand and say, 'isn't that just wonderful! I'm Mrs. Scruggs, the cleaning woman. Welcome to the Point.'

It was such a cheery welcome, so open and warm, that it chased away the ghosts that had been haunting me a moment before, as the sunlight chases away the shadows of night.

'I'm pleased to meet you,' I said, and meant it. 'Alan has mentioned you.'

'I come once a week,' she said. 'To each of the houses. Tomorrow I'll do Farroday's place. It's little but he makes such a mess of things, it takes me as long there as it does here. Then the next day I do Mrs. Denver's. The other Mrs. Denver that is to say. Hers is easy. She keeps it spotless herself, I don't know why she bothers having me at all, but I don't complain, because the money comes in handy.'

She delivered her remarks in long phrases, taking deep breaths of air between them, as if she were in a hurry to get everything said. One got the feeling she would, if encouraged, say a great deal. I had an impression that the news of Alan's marriage would not long remain secret. She glanced about as if she would like right now to get to a phone and share it with someone.

'Had you known the master long?' she asked with a sideways glance as she put her purse and lunch bag aside.

'We only met on his leave this time,' I said, and saw how she savored this bit of information. 'I'm afraid we gave everybody a surprise.'

She did not overlook this hint, and she was as willing to dispense information as she was to garner it. 'Your mother-in-law, you mean?' she said, nodding. 'I'll bet you could have knocked her over with a feather. But don't you fret about that sort of thing. She keeps a close eye on her son, I've noticed that, but it seems to me that he's pretty independent, his own man, if you know what I mean. And a fine young man, too, I've worked for some as wasn't, I can tell you, but Mr. Denver's been as nice as nice could be.'

She paused, giving me a long look up and down that was intended without subterfuge to size me up. 'Well,' she said again, and her eyes gleamed.

She set about her work then, and I had things of my own that I wanted to do, so I left her. It was nearly lunchtime when I finished what I was doing. I came downstairs thinking of the meal I was going to prepare. Much as I would like to regale Alan with gourmet delights, it was going to be rather a simple lunch.

He had already warned me, and I had observed for myself yesterday, that supplies were a bit low until I was able to make a shopping trip. There were no markets nearer than the town of Lompoc, some thirty-five miles distant. Shopping trips were a once a week business, and needed to be carefully planned so that no necessities were overlooked. The forgotten item could be a weeklong nuisance until the next regular visit, unless one wanted to make extra and expensive trips into town.

Because he had been preparing to go on leave, Alan had kept his purchases minimal on his last few shopping trips, putting in a few canned and frozen items, and in quantities for one, not for two. I would have to make a shopping trip soon, and quite a major one.

Mrs. Scruggs had brought her own lunch and although I invited her to lunch with us, she declined. 'It seems to me that you didn't get much of a honeymoon anyway,' she said. 'I don't suppose your hubby would appreciate my butting into your lunchtime.'

Instead, she took her sandwiches and thermos of hot chocolate out to the courtyard to eat in the sun. 'There's a table and chairs out there,' she explained. 'Mr. Denver never wanted to use them, but now that you're here, I'll get them out and clean them. You might want to sit out there from time to time and I don't mind having my lunches there in good weather, if it's all right with you.'

Alone in the kitchen, I looked over what was available and began to prepare lunch. Alan's taste ran to simple, hearty fare, for the most part. I had prepared a few meals for him at my apartment and knew pretty well how to please him.

I was peeling potatoes when he came in. He put his arms about me in a fierce hug, kissing the back of my neck.

'I missed you,' he said in a hoarse whisper.

'It's only been a couple of hours,' I said, laughing.

'It seems like an eternity.' He turned me around to kiss my mouth. I forgot all about the sharp knife in my hand and returned his kiss warmly.

Of such carelessness are accidents born. I felt a sudden, brief twinge of pain and realized I had run my finger across the blade of the knife.

'How stupid,' I said, 'I've cut myself.'

It was only a superficial cut but it was bleeding profusely, a scarlet train running across the palm of my hand. 'Are there any bandages in the bathroom?'

He didn't answer and when I looked at him, it was a shock. I don't know what I had expected — perhaps amusement at my clumsiness or even annoyance, but I was unprepared for the look of horror on his face. He stared wide-eyed at the cut on my fingers, his mouth open. It might have been a severed limb he was staring at, so violent was his reaction, and he transmitted his horror to me, so that I too stood frozen, unable to speak.

'Oh, God,' he cried, a groan of agony that sounded from the very depths of his soul. He turned suddenly and ran from the room, stumbling as if he were blind.

'Alan,' I cried. I grabbed a towel from the rack by the sink, wrapping it about my hand, and went after him.

I found him at the rear of the house, leaning his head against the cool stone of the building, his back to me.

'Alan?' I said, putting out a hand to touch him gently.

He turned slowly. He was no longer horror-stricken but he was pale and drawn, as if he had just undergone some terrible ordeal.

'I'm all right now,' he said, breathing hard.

'What was it, darling?' I asked. 'Something terrified you.'

'It was just . . . ' He paused, as if even the word was difficult for him. 'The blood.'

I didn't know what to say. It was hard to conceive that any man would be so horrified at the blood from that small cut on my finger.

'It's all right, really.' He put an arm about me and pulled me to him, but I had a feeling it was he who wanted comforting and not the other way around. I wanted to ask him to explain. I felt there must surely be more to it.

The experience had frightened me too, however. I held my silence, and was glad that it was over.

* * *

45

Those first few days were days of discovery, so crowded full with new delights that I had only the faintest awareness of the little notes of discord creeping into them.

If I had taken time to contemplate them, to put them into the right perspective, I might have begun to suspect much sooner that something was amiss, but I did not. As a result, I spent those days blissfully happy. Only occasionally did I have troubled thoughts, and then I did not long dwell upon them.

The house alone kept me occupied for a few days. It was a big house, although the largeness of the rooms meant that there were fewer rooms than would have been supposed from a look at the outside.

The house was built around the courtyard. One entire end was the large living room, the back of which overlooked the ocean, as did the dining room and the kitchen. The center facing the courtyard was the wide entryway, and at the opposite end of the house, in the other wing, was a large reading room, lined with books.

'We do a lot of reading here,' Alan said when I commented on this room. 'Don't worry, you'll get the habit too.'

It was a habit, in fact, which I'd had most of my life, and the presence of so many books provided me with the anticipation of many happy hours.

The bedrooms were upstairs. Our bedroom and a guest bedroom were side by side, each with its own bath. In the wing above the reading room was a charming nursery. I liked the idea that Alan had slept there as a child. The figured wallpaper with its colorful Mother Goose characters had faded and I looked forward to papering it anew for our own child one day.

The door to what I assumed was another guest bedroom in the opposite wing proved to be locked. I looked in the kitchen where the various keys to the house and the lighthouse hung, but I did not find one that fit that particular door. Nor was Alan able to give me much help.

'I can't imagine why it should be locked,' he said, showing no great interest. 'But it's only another bedroom, and we don't need it, so why not just leave it locked?'

'You may know a great deal about ocean currents and lighthouses,' I told him, 'but you obviously don't understand a woman's curiosity. From the moment I found that door locked, I've been dying to know what dire secrets you have hidden away there.'

'I'm afraid you'll only be disappointed. Unless Mrs. Scruggs has been hiding something there — but that's probably your answer.'

I gave him a scornful look. 'You can't really think Mrs. Scruggs has something hidden there. And if she did, being the gossip that she is, she'd be the first to tell me about it anyway.'

He laughed at that suggestion. 'No, what I meant was, she has a key. She has a complete set of keys to all the buildings. Why don't you have her unlock the room when she comes next week?'

'I guess that's all I can do,' I said a bit reluctantly.

After a time, however, I decided it was just as well I had to wait a week. A locked door gave a certain element of mystery to the house. Once the door was opened and Alan was proved right, as I was certain he would be, the romantic possibilities would be gone. I was rather glad now to tease myself with the door and I cast searching glances in that direction whenever I passed by.

Other than the house, I had the entire coast to explore, as far as I wanted to ramble, a dizzying stretch of jagged rocks and glistening cliffs wet with sea spray in either direction.

On my third day in the house, I decided I ought to repay Mrs. Denver's visit. I told Alan, and said, 'I suppose the best way is to go along the coast.'

He looked a bit doubtful. 'That's a treacherous path. The rocks get wet and slippery and sometimes you have to scramble right over them.'

'Your mother makes it all right.'

'She's used to it.'

A little annoyed that he thought me less capable than his mother, I said, 'She wasn't always,' and considered it settled that I would go by the sea path.

When I was actually on my way, however, I began to think my impulsiveness was a bit ill-advised. There was, in fact, no real path at all except in a few spots where one had been worn through the grass. For the most part, I simply followed the coastline, knowing that it would eventually take me to Mrs. Denver's cottage.

More often than not I found myself walking cautiously across slick rocks worn smooth by centuries of wind and spray. At one point I had to choose between a long walk — just how long I could not tell — around an outcropping of rock, or a rough, dangerous-looking climb over. I chose the latter course, but by the time I had reached the top and firmer ground, I had decided I would go home by the road. I wondered at the ease with which Mrs. Denver made this trip, but I felt it unwise of me to challenge her superiority.

After about a mile, I stopped in a sheltered cove to catch my breath and to enjoy the view of life in the little tidal pool, like a miniature sea, that had been created there.

At first glance it appeared still, but as I waited and watched, I began to make out first one and then another form of life. An anemone stirred. What I had taken to be a stone strolled nonchalantly about. Something peeked hesitantly out from beneath a shelf of rock. In a short time, I saw that the pool was swarming with life.

Suddenly the crest of a wave cleared the rock on which I was standing, splashing my feet and lashing out at the tidal basin. When it had retreated, the entire scene had changed. Lives had been swapped for others. Nothing was the same.

★   ★   ★

Although I was able to make do with the stores on hand in the house, it soon became necessary that I make a shopping trip into Lompoc.

'I'd go with you,' Alan said, 'but I don't think it would be fair of me to take off so soon again and leave Farroday with the work.'

'I understand,' I assured him. 'Anyway,

I'm sure your mother will welcome a chance to go. I'll check and see if she would like to make the trip with me.'

As it turned out, she had chosen that day to bake bread, a project already well under way when I called on her. I ended up driving to Lompoc by myself.

Not, of course, that this was such a great or perilous journey. It was thirty-five miles on good roads, with no danger of highwaymen. I made the trip without incident, and while my principal reason for coming had been groceries, I decided to take a few extra minutes to stroll through the town.

The town had a typically California look and feel, and after a few days in the isolation of the Point, it was pleasant to have the sight and sound of other people about me, bustling to and fro. I could see that in time these visits would be very welcome.

I remembered that only a handful of the people I knew had been informed of my marriage, and seeing a stationery store, I stopped to buy some writing paper. The saleslady studied me with frank curiosity while she took care of my few purchases. As she was wrapping them, she ventured to say, 'You must be the new Mrs. Denver.'

Mrs. Scruggs had been busy, I thought, but I did not mind. 'Yes,' I said, 'I hadn't realized my fame had preceded me.'

'We don't have a lot to talk about up here,' she said honestly. 'And a wedding is always news. Especially when it's someone like that nice husband of yours. I felt so badly about that business with the other Mrs. Denver.'

'Alan's mother, you mean?'

She answered absent-mindedly. 'No, I mean Alan's first . . . ' She paused then, because she had looked at me as she handed me the package and she must have seen my surprise. It was an awkward pause. She plainly did not know what to say. She thrust the package at me almost angrily.

'Well, I hope you'll be very happy at the Point. Excuse me,' and with that she bustled off toward the sanctuary of a back room.

I stood for a moment in puzzlement,

trying to think what she had meant. Alan's first . . . wife? But that was ridiculous. Not that I thought for a moment Alan had told me everything about his past. For one thing, there simply hadn't been time enough. We were still learning about one another every day.

A previous marriage, however, was not the sort of thing a man would neglect to mention, or put off indefinitely. If Alan had been married before, he would surely have mentioned it to me prior to our own marriage.

Wouldn't he?

I went to the market and did my shopping. I noted that several people watched me and were as curious as the woman in the stationery store had been, but I no longer felt inclined to talk to them. I felt as if they knew things I did not know. I seemed to be at a disadvantage, and I felt a bit cross as a result.

Driving back to the Point, I tried to think again what the woman in the store had been trying to say. ' . . . The other Mrs. Denver.' Something had happened that she felt badly about.

All right, what could 'another Mrs. Denver' mean? The answer occurred to me out of the blue. Of course, Alan must have a brother, who had a wife to whom something unpleasant had happened.

Only, hadn't Alan told me he was an only child? Or had I just assumed that?

Or had Alan's father married more than once? That was a distinct possibility, and the sort of thing that might not have been mentioned yet simply because it had not come into the conversation.

I took a corner too fast and had to remind myself I was driving home, not running a race.

No, the most obvious answer was that Alan had been married before and had chosen for whatever reason not to tell me about it.

Having reached this conclusion, I still had some fifteen miles to drive, during which time I could seethe, so that I was in a fair state when I reached the house.

Alan and Farroday were busy repaint-ing the exterior of the lighthouse. I did not want to create a quarrel in front of Alan's co-worker, so I had to curb my impulse to confront Alan at once, and instead had to wait for the opportunity.

I did not have to wait long, however. Soon after I got home, Alan came in to see how my trip had gone. Another time I might have been flattered, but I was not in a romantic frame of mind just now.

He tried to give me a kiss. I dodged it coolly and it landed on my ear instead of my lips as intended.

'Hey,' he said, surprised, 'is something wrong?'

'Since you ask,' I said drily, 'something is. I would like to know why you did not inform me of the first Mrs. Denver?'

'The first . . . ?' He looked uncomprehending. 'You mean my mother?'

'I mean,' I said, beginning to lose a bit of wind from my sails as the thought crept into my mind that perhaps I had jumped to the wrong conclusion, 'your first wife.'

'My first wife?' the puzzlement on his face gave way to annoyance and then anger. 'What the devil do you mean? You are my first wife.'

My face went crimson. I suddenly

wished the ground might swallow me up and spare me the embarrassment looming before me.

'You mean you haven't been married before?' I asked in a tiny voice.

He slammed his hand down hard upon the counter top, making the dishes in the cupboard rattle. He was angry, quite angry, and obviously making a great effort to control that anger.

'Don't you think that's the sort of thing a man would tell his wife?' he asked in a dry voice.

I did not see at the time that he hadn't really answered my question. All I could think of just then was that Alan was angry — justifiably so, it seemed.

'I did think,' I stammered. 'That's why . . . Oh, Alan, I'm so sorry.'

I threw myself into his arms and buried my face against his chest. After a moment his arms came about me and I knew the storm had passed.

'All right,' he said, patting my shoulders, 'now tell me what that was all about.'

I told him about the woman in the

store in town and the remark that had upset me.

'And I jumped to the wrong conclusion,' I finished lamely. 'I'm sorry, darling, truly I am. You have every right to be furious with me for not trusting you.'

He bent down to kiss my forehead. His anger had gone as quickly as it had come, but it had given me a glimpse of a side to his nature that I hadn't seen before.

'Okay, let's just forget the whole thing, shall we?' he said. 'Now, I'd better get back to work before Farroday thinks I'm shirking my share of the chores. See you later.'

As he was going out, however, something occurred to me and I called after him, 'But, Alan, what Mrs. Denver was that woman referring to?'

'I have no idea.' He went out, letting the door slam shut after him.

I should have known then, of course.

3

Looking back, there is no specific point at which I can say I began to suspect the truth. It was more a gradual thing, a growing awareness that things were not as rosy and bright as I had been seeing them.

I had accepted what my husband told me — that he had not been married before. He said he did not know what Mrs. Denver the woman in the shop in town had been referring to.

A part of me believed him, but in some other, less romantic part of my mind, the questions lingered, beginning to grow and multiply.

Despite these signs of discord, the days that followed my visit into town were pleasant for the most part. I was in love, newly married to a handsome, affectionate husband. Even the wild setting, despite its threatening aspect, added to the romance I was enjoying. It was difficult to be afraid of ghosts when they remained just that, vague shadows, and when the real world remained so enchanting.

But the ghosts were there. Like the angry waves of the ocean, they throbbed and surged in the distance, waiting to lash out at me. Their whispers blended with the murmur of the sea, and they spoke of things better unheard.

Sometimes I thought I knew of what they spoke. It seemed to me that they spoke of the loneliness and the isolation of this place, that they waited for a weak moment to close in upon me, and oppress me. Sometimes I thought they spoke of the past, of Alan's past, of which I knew so little. Sometimes I thought that they, like Mrs. Denver, resented my presence here.

'You'll just have to be patient with her,' Alan said when I broached the subject of his mother. 'When you've been here a while you will understand how possessive one becomes of things and of the few people around. Farroday is like a mother hen with me sometimes. It's being cut off from other people.'

'Maybe your mother ought to leave the Point,' I said thoughtfully. 'There's really no need for her to stay here by herself, in that lonely cottage.'

'Where would she go? She hasn't anyone else, no family or close friends. After all these years, she'd be just as lonely anywhere else.'

He was right. I sighed and said, 'Yes, I suppose so.'

He put an arm about me and kissed me. 'She'll come around, don't worry. She likes you, I'm sure of it. I predict the two of you will be the closest of friends in a short while.'

'I hope you're right.' Inwardly, I felt less confident. Thus far my efforts to establish a friendship with his mother had met with a complete lack of success.

'I know I am,' he said. He gave me a squeeze and went out into the night. It was storming, and his turn for duty. I stood at the door, watching him make his way along the cliff to the steps that led down.

The wind blew the rain in heavy sheets.

I felt nervous about his going out in such weather, but I kept my anxiety to myself. Such storms were common here and he had to be out in them. I could only undermine his confidence by expressing a lot of womanly fears. Better I conceal them as best I could and put on a cheerful face for his benefit.

Apparently sensing that I was watching, he turned at the steps and gave a wave of his hand before starting down. I waved back. Then he was gone.

I went inside, closing the door on the howling winds. The house suddenly seemed larger and emptier than before. Tonight the world seemed angry, and although it was relatively quiet in the house, it was an uneasy quiet.

I tried to read, but my thoughts kept drifting from the book in my hands. I went to the stereo and selected some music. The lovely strains of Mendelssohn filled the room, that quite un-Latin symphony he called the Italian. He had seen the sea, the Italian sea, as 'like a meadow of pure ether as you gaze at it.' How different that was from the sea here.

Mendelssohn, however, had remained a German composer in Italy. Was that not, in a sense, my problem here? Wasn't I remaining Karen of Los Angeles, here in this entirely different place? I was seeing everything from the outside looking in, and it looked foreign and strange to me, sometimes charming, sometimes mysterious or even frightening. How different might it look if I were to let myself become a part of it, without reserve?

Yes, there was part of the trouble. I had not quite gotten over a certain reserve as icy in its own way as that of Alan's mother. Despite my love for Alan, and my desire to make a success of our marriage, I was still a stranger to it all, still outside looking in. Worse, I was looking through romance-clouded glasses.

Yet, when I tried to see more clearly, the images refused to come. The simple fact was: I knew no more about Alan than I had when I married him. I knew he was a person who was essentially thoughtful and pleasant, although subject to strong emotions.

Looking at him now, however, he

seemed like a man without a past. At least I did not know his past. And looking at it in this new, colder light, I had the feeling that he had evaded my questions about it.

I had accepted that as modesty, and a desire to talk about me rather than about himself. In fact, though, he was mysterious.

I recalled the scar on his forehead. He did not remember, he said, where it came from. He had a violent aversion to the sight of blood and no reason to explain it. He did not remember his dreams. He did not know to whom the woman in Lompoc had referred.

It suddenly seemed to me that my husband had avoided providing answers to any question that I asked him.

The symphony had ended. The silence that had been hovering in the corners of the room rushed in upon me. Feeling ill-at-ease, I got up and went into the kitchen to get myself a glass of milk. I busied myself there for a few moments, trying not to go back to my previous train of thought.

The thoughts kept coming, however.

Back in the living room, the fire I had lit earlier was still burning low. It seemed to be trying to dispel the gloom that pervaded the house this night.

I stood before it for a moment, watching the flames lick at the wood. A sudden tapping made me start. At first I saw nothing. I was looking in the direction of the hall, and of the door.

A movement caught my eye. I looked at the window instead, and saw a hand, seemingly disembodied. It gestured once, as if beckoning me.

Then it was gone.

I felt the skin on the back of my neck stir as if something were crawling over it. That ghostly hand had come and gone so quickly that for a moment I had no thoughts regarding it. When reaction did come, it came in the form of terror. I had seen one of the ghosts said to haunt the Point!

'Don't be a fool,' I told myself. The hand that I had seen had been real. Someone was outside in the storm. Perhaps it was a lost traveler, or someone whose boat had gone aground on the rocks. Certainly it was someone in distress. There was no mistake in the gesture it had given, a gesture of summons.

No longer frightened for myself, but for the hapless person outside, I ran to the front door, flinging it open. The light that I flicked on seemed barely able to penetrate the darkness.

'Hello,' I cried, stepping out into the night. The rain beat against me at once, icy fingers of water seizing me in a chill grasp, but no reply came to my call.

I was quickly drenched. My hair hung wetly about my face, and my clothes were soaked. I stepped back into the house, grabbing a slicker from the rack there and slipping into it. Storms were frequent here, and rainwear was always kept easily accessible by the door.

Still there was no sign of my phantom visitor. The courtyard was empty. The window at which I had seen the hand was at the side of the house.

Not until I had a rounded the corner of the house did I think of a flashlight. The light in the courtyard had seemed dim, but now I was in darkness without relief. I paused, wondering if I should run back inside for light.

At that moment a flash of lightning broke upon the scene. I had a glimpse of a figure in the distance, leaping from one black rock to another at the very edge of the cliff above the ocean. It was so brief but I could not be certain a moment later that I had really seen a person and not just another shadow that my imagination had shaped into a human likeness.

'Hello, where are you?' I cried, cupping my hands about my mouth, but the wind seized the words and flung them high and away. I might as well have whispered.

The lightning flashed again. This time I saw nothing on the rocks before the darkness enveloped me. The wind caught at my slicker, sending it billowing behind me.

I ran toward the rocks. Whoever was there must have been frightened, or even dazed. He had run from me blindly, and perhaps had fallen upon the rocks. I did not like that spot toward which I ran. Those crags hung out over the edge, hovering suspended above the rocks below and the pounding sea. A fall from the ledge above would be a fall to one's death. Even in the light of a pleasant day it had given me a chill to stand ever so briefly upon the smaller of the huge boulders.

I slipped once on the wet earth, nearly falling to the ground. I was gasping for breath, chilled to the bone in the brief space of time in which I had been in the rain. I heard, or thought I heard, a cry, like a distant scream, but it was impossible to say whether it was a scream or the wind calling me on, urging me to the rocks.

Yes, there it was again, cry, a wail of terror, it seemed to me. I reached the rocky surface, scrambling upward. The wind here was fierce, threatening to send me off balance, toppling over.

I reached the top. The rock had been worn smooth here. There was a platform of a foot or two, and then a deep crevice that separated it from the next mammoth boulder. Just to my left, only inches away, the surface ended abruptly, and beyond was space and sky, and a drop of hundreds of feet to jagged rocks and thrashing waves below.

For a moment it seemed as if I were being drawn toward that end of the earth. I took a step, falteringly, and another.

The spell passed. I caught my breath, flinging my head back so that the rain beat harshly against my upturned face.

A woman screamed.

I turned, too suddenly. My foot slipped on the wet surface. I may have cried out. I did not remember. I came down scrabbling and grabbing out for some hold that was not there. I hit the wet rock hard, skidding, sliding downward, toward the edge. I rolled once or twice, and saw what looked to be blood on the rock.

Somehow I stopped, at the very edge. My head lay to the side, and the edge of rock creased my cheek, while my eyes looked through the rain to the sea. One arm and one leg dangled over the precipice. I dared not move for fear of sliding over. I dared not breathe. I lay in horror and contemplated what must happen next — the slow slipping over, toppling, falling . . .

'Don't move.' It was Alan's voice, sharp and loud, and so authoritative it would have frozen the most hysterical soul motionless.

I sensed, rather than saw him bending over me. I was afraid even to move my eyes to look at him, for fear that tiny movement would seal my fate.

One hand grasped my wrist.

'Don't move,' he said again. I did see him then, leaning over me, grasping as well the hand that dangled in the air past the edge of rock.

Then he was lifting me, pulling me hard toward him. The rock scraped at my leg painfully, as if trying to seize back its prey, but Alan had me and held me. In a moment I was in his arms, flinging myself against him and sobbing aloud with relief.

'Darling, Alan,' I cried. 'Thank god you saw me.'

'It's all right,' he said patting me until I was past the worst of it. Then he lifted me easily in his strong arms and carried me back toward the house.

His mother appeared suddenly, peering

down at me with anxious eyes. 'Is she . . . ?'

'She's all right,' he said. 'Just a little shaken up. Get the door, will you?'

He carried me in, depositing me gently on the sofa before the still-burning fire. It was with a shock that I realized it had been only a minute or two since I had gone out into the storm. It seemed an eternity ago that I had stood before this very fire and heard that tapping at the window.

I struggled to a sitting position. 'Someone's out there,' I cried.

'Out there?' Alan had been examining my bleeding leg. He looked up into my face.

'I saw someone,' I said.

'A man?' Alan's mother asked. She had stooped beside him to look at the cuts on my leg.

'I suppose so,' I said. Then, realizing how vague that sounded, I said, 'I saw a hand. It tapped at the glass, at that window.'

They exchanged glances. I had the impression they did not believe me, and that angered me.

'I thought someone was lost, or hurt,' I went on, more sharply than I should have. 'I went out to see. I thought I saw someone on the rocks.'

I paused. Even at that time, I had not been altogether certain. Now, in a warm, well lighted room, it sounded foolish.

'When I got there, there was no one. But I heard someone screaming.'

'I screamed,' Mrs. Denver said. 'I saw you on the rocks. I thought you were going to . . . ' She did not finish the sentence.

'I saw you too,' Alan said. 'I couldn't imagine why you were out at all, and in this storm, up on those rocks. I started toward you, but you fell before I got there. You scared the devil out of me.'

'I had a few thrills out of it to myself,' I said, attempting a laugh that came out a bit insecurely. Something came to me suddenly and without thinking I said, 'Alan, you haven't even noticed all the blood . . . ' I caught myself.

He looked at me a bit strangely, and down at my knee, which was still bleeding. For a moment he seemed to pale, but he gave a shaky laugh of his own, and met my eyes again.

'I was so worried about you, I never even thought about it,' he said, getting up. 'I'd better wash that. I'll get some hot water.'

He went out, leaving me with his mother. She was turned toward the window, staring. I followed her gaze, half expecting to see that beckoning hand again but the glass was dark and there was no hand now.

'I did see someone there,' I said.

'A hand,' she said, sounding oddly sad. 'A beckoning hand.'

My heart skipped a beat. 'Yes, it was beckoning. But how did you know?'

She did not answer for a long moment. Finally, bending down to examine my leg again, she said, 'Oh, other people have seen beckoning hands. I myself have seen things on these cliffs that ordinary people would scoff at.'

Alan came back then, with hot water in a basin and a towel over his arm. He set himself to dressing the wounds on my leg. Although I could see it cost him some effort, he had managed to overcome his revulsion at the sight of blood. I was grateful, yet at the same time troubled because I still did not know what had caused it.

His mother went to the kitchen to fix something warm for us to drink. When she had gone, her comments lingered in the room with me, like the presence of a grim ghost.

★   ★   ★

There was more fussing over me, until my leg was bandaged and I had been soaked in a hot bath and tucked in bed. Alan had to return to work, and, despite my protests, his mother insisted on remaining with me.

'I'm all right, really,' I said, propped up in bed with a cup of hot chocolate on the table beside me.

'Nonsense,' Mrs. Denver replied, 'you've had a bad scare. Look at yourself, you're still as white as that sheet. And I don't mind staying over, really I don't. I felt restless anyway tonight. That's what prompted me to come over for a visit.'

'Lucky thing you did,' Alan said. To me, he said, 'Look, honey, I'll be knocking off about midnight. If she wants to go home then, I can drive her and save her the walk, all right?'

'Well, if you don't mind babysitting,' I said, yielding to their combined insistence.

'You just put everything out of your mind,' she said, 'and get some sleep. I'll be right here if you need me.'

I could hardly think I would need her — though it was true, I was still a bit shaken but I was not planning on going back out again, and I was capable of getting around, so I was not really an invalid. Still, I saw no point in arguing. I thanked her graciously, settling myself in to sleep, which I did soon after they left the room.

I woke late in the night. My leg had begun to ache and I got up to take an aspirin. A glance at the clock told me it was nearly two in the morning, but Alan was not in bed.

I saw lights below and started downstairs. As I got nearer I heard voices in the kitchen, Alan's and his mother's. They were chatting and I heard her laugh. She sounded so carefree and happy, so unlike the reserved, cool woman I knew, that the sound gave me pause.

They were drinking coffee at the kitchen table, a plate before Alan that held the remnants of bacon and eggs. Obviously she had fixed him breakfast when he finished work. I paused in the kitchen doorway, thinking again how happy she looked. She was in her element now, and it was an element, I realized, in which I was quite literally an intruder.

She looked up and saw me in the doorway. She had been laughing at something Alan had said, but I saw a mask, as it were, slip over her face, so swiftly and so subtly that one might almost have failed to see it.

'I hope we didn't wake you,' she said, and if I had not seen that mask slip into place, I would have thought her expression and her manner perfectly friendly — but I knew they were not.

'I went for an aspirin,' I said, feeling oddly guilty at intruding on their conversation. 'And I saw you weren't in bed . . . '

'We got started talking over old times,' he said, glancing at the clock on the wall, 'and I guess we didn't realize how the time was passing.'

'Heavens, is it two?' Mrs. Denver said, casting a look at the clock too. 'I think I'll scoot back to the house, unless you feel you need me here.'

'I'm all right, really I am,' I assured her. 'Of course you're welcome to stay if you want.'

She glanced at the window. 'It's stopped raining. Anyway, I don't want to make a pest of myself.'

Alan came to slip an arm about my waist. 'No danger of that,' he said. 'We're always happy to have you here, aren't we, darling?'

'Of course,' I said, and tried to mean it. They exchanged smiles. I thought of the old times they had been discussing so happily before, old times which were a part of the past in which I had no place, and of which I knew so very little. I suddenly felt like an outsider, despite

Alan's arm about me.

They went toward the front door. 'You go ahead,' I said, 'I'm going to pour myself a glass of milk.'

I got my milk and was coming to join them at the front of the house, when I heard Mrs. Denver say, 'I hope you haven't made a mistake, dear.' I paused inside the door, where they wouldn't see me.

'What sort of mistake?' Alan asked.

'Bringing Karen here. She seems to have a strong imagination, and you know how dangerous that can be here.'

Alan's reply was lost to me. I turned the kitchen light out and joined them as noisily as I could.

I suppose it was at this point that the sadness really began for me. At first, it was minor, like the verge of a pain that has not yet quite began to hurt but that soon will, and will become monstrous.

★ ★ ★

I awakened a few nights later to find that Alan was not in bed. Had it not been for that earlier incident, I might just have supposed he had gone for a drink of water, but a sense of dread had been haunting me. I sat bolt upright. 'Alan?' I called. There was no answer.

I slipped from bed, feeling for robe and slippers. At first, I could not quite spell out in my mind what made things seem so ominous, but when I started along the hall, I realized that there were no lights on downstairs.

Surely if Alan had simply been unable to sleep and had gone downstairs, he would have switched on a light somewhere.

'Alan, are you down here?' Still no reply.

I stood in the lower hall, listening. The house spoke to me in faint creaks and groans. The ocean whispered just beyond of the range of my hearing.

There is a knowledge that comes to us from no external accumulation of evidence, but instead springs from some inner source of information. Call it instinct, clairvoyance, call it what you will.

I knew the house was empty. There were no answering vibrations of life, none of the warmth that emanates from another person nearby.

Even as I realized this truth, another came into my mind. A cold wind was blowing the length of the hall, not the drafts that I had come to realize were common to the house at night, but more than that. This was the wind of out-of-doors, as foreign here as some wild animal suddenly brought inside to live as a house pet, a distant wind that had come from beyond the horizon, that had traveled distant seas and found itself now in this foreign place. It hastened down the hall, as if it traveled on limited time. It touched me with tentative, mildly curious fingers, as I might run a hand over the marble columns at Delphi, because they were strange to me, and not of my world or experience.

There was no reason for the panic that suddenly assailed me. There were a hundred reasons why Alan might get up in the night and go out, leaving the door open for the night winds to discover and explore.

Farroday may have come for him. The alarm, which automatically warned them if the lights failed, might have awakened him. He might simply have suffered a bout of insomnia, and finding himself unable to sleep, he may have felt an urge to stand and watch the ocean.

These and a score of other explanations came to me later, when I looked back upon this in the cold light of day. None of them crossed my mind at that time, however. I reacted to the night and chill and aloneness with panic.

'Alan,' I cried aloud, and ran toward the back door. It stood open to the night. I thought of the mysterious hand that had beckoned me, almost to my death. Had it, or something, beckoned him from his sleep, and to what destination?

The wind caught me in its grip, aroused to fascination by my sudden swift movement. For a moment it held me just beyond the door, and I could not move.

In that moment, I saw Alan. He was walking along the cliff, at the very edge, seeming to look for something, but whether something on the ground, or something far below in the sea, I could not say.

I almost cried out to him, but the foghorn lowed just then, sounding cautious as if it did not want to startle him, and nor did I. He was at the very edge of the earth, so close that a single false step could send him plummeting downward to the sharp rocks below.

I breathed deeply, willing myself to be calm. He turned once in my direction, and I waited for some call of recognition, a sign of greeting, but none came. He turned away again, as if I were not even there.

I began to walk toward him, cautiously, because I did not want to startle him. I had already guessed the truth, and when I was close enough to see his face, I knew my guess had been right.

He was asleep.

I nearly panicked. I thought of him walking unknowingly along these cliffs, where one false step might carry one across the line that separated the realm of life from the kingdom of death. A cry of horror rose in my throat, and I clapped a hand over my mouth.

Fate mocked me, though. As I stood in a frozen silence, the wind, growing impatient with our little drama, seized the door of the house, and sent it crashing shut.

I whirled toward the sound, half expecting to see some figure from another realm, the creature of the beckoning hand, the ghost of some long-ago-drowned a sailor. There was only the night and the wind.

Alan seemed not to have heard. He had come to the bit of land that pointed like a finger into the distance and stood looking out to sea. I could not even guess what phantom ships held his eye. Perhaps he heard the cries of sailors in anguish, or saw masts splintering as ships ran up on the rocks. Perhaps he saw the rotted hulks, carried on the waves, coming in to haunt the beach. Whatever the ghosts that haunted these cliffs, he was among them now. No world of the living held his eye and bade him listen.

I trembled as I came nearer to him, and to the edge. I could not help but remember my own nightmare experience on the rocks. Now the roles were reversed, but with a difference I was too well aware of. If he started to fall, or even to jump, I hadn't the strength to hold him back.

I reached his side. Still he had given no sign that he was aware of my presence. He stood as before, looking out over the ocean.

I put a hand as gently as I could upon his arm, and said very softly, 'Alan.'

He turned, his eyes open. For a moment he looked at me in a strange, uncomprehending way, as if unable to grasp what he saw.

Then he smiled, and in that place, in that time, there was something eerie about his smile. He spoke but he neither smiled nor spoke to me. Whomever he saw before him, it was not me.

'Emily,' he said. 'You've come back.'

4

Emily. That name meant nothing to me then. It was only a name, a name from the dream world in which he then journeyed.

A name and rose point lace. Upon what simple things was my house of fear built. Simple, and lovely.

'Alan, darling, it's me,' I said giving his arm a gentle shake. I stepped instinctively away from the cliff, tugging at his arm, and to my relief, he came with me.

'Karen?' He was awake now, the dream world fleeing, already gone with the wisps of fog that drifted about us, riding on a gust of wind that whipped my robe about my cold legs.

'It's all right, darling,' I said, with a calm that surprised even myself. 'Come with me.'

I led him a step or two further away from the cliff and began to breathe more easily again. He hesitated, looking in puzzlement about him.

'What's happened?' he asked. I could see from his expression that he truly had no idea of how he had gotten where he was.

'You've had a dream,' I said. 'Come inside, please, I'll explain there. Please, darling, it's cold out here.'

He came, and of course by the time we had gotten inside and I had leaned in weary relief against the closed door, he had guessed the truth.

'Was I walking in my sleep?' he asked.

I nodded. Now that it was over, I was not altogether certain I could trust my voice. My legs felt as if they were made of rubber.

He suddenly saw how frightened I was, and I was grateful that he found his strange behavior less important than my comfort.

'Hey, you look awful,' he said. He gathered me up in his arms, comforting me. 'It's okay,' he said again and again. 'It's all over now.'

He was himself, and in charge, the strong husband comforting his weak, frightened wife, reassuring her, taking her back to bed.

It wasn't until he was asleep again, and I was staring wide-eyed at the ceiling, that things slipped back into their right perspective.

Alan was a sleepwalker, in this, the most frightening of all places for such an ailment. I had found him on the cliffs, and awakened him before any harm had been done — this time.

How could I doubt that he would do the same again? Surely there would be another time when he would rise from his bed, walk to the cliffs, and . . . and what? Would he go over them? I had no idea, but the danger was certainly there. Those cliffs were dangerous enough at night for a man wide-awake.

Beside me, Allan moved slightly and I froze into immobility, fearful of waking him, fearful more of rousing him to that state between sleep and wakefulness in which I had so recently seen him.

Was he, like Lady Macbeth, driven by some crime from the past? I felt a pang of guilt at even thinking such a thing, but there it was, come unbidden, and it would not go away.

What had called him from his bed, summoned him to the cliffs?

I knew the answer to that question, though. He had already told me himself. It had scarcely registered, because at the moment I had his safety on my mind, and afterward had been the relief that it was over.

Emily. The name came back to me now. Who was Emily? Had he mentioned anyone of that name to me? I searched my memory, with no success.

I decided in the morning I would ask his mother who Emily was. It did not even occur to me to wonder why I had decided to ask her, and not Alan. It did not cross my mind that I had already taken it for granted he would give me no answer, and that I must search for the truth.

I tried to sleep but I couldn't. Each slight movement in his sleep brought my eyes wide open. I finally gave up hope of sleep and prayed for the night to end. I wanted light. I wanted morning, but the gradual graying of dawn did not make things better. Still I lay, my open eyes aching.

At last, as if in sleep he sensed my

discomfort, Alan turned and put an arm tenderly over me. The warmth of his body drove out the chill that enveloped me. I moved gratefully into the circle of his embrace, gave myself up to his protection, and slept.

I woke late. The light had gone from gray to golden and I was alone. I sat up, alarmed, but at once I told myself that it was daylight now, and late, and he was undoubtedly at work.

Despite what had happened during the night, Alan was in a good humor when he came in for lunch. I suppose I expected him to feel as uneasy about the incident as I still felt, but he dismissed it as of no particular consequence.

'Of course,' I said, 'you slept through the worst of it.'

'I guess so,' he said, laughing. 'Look at it this way, what's to be frightened of? I was out by the cliffs, but I go there all the time anyway. My eyes were open, weren't they?'

'They were when you turned to look at me. Only, I don't think you were really seeing me at all.'

'What else could I have been seeing?'

'I don't know. Maybe some other woman. Someone from your past.'

He shook his head. 'Not a chance. There weren't any.' He winked at me so that I was both pleased and aggravated.

'Oh, Alan, be serious. This is important. There must have been at least one woman before me, someone of importance.'

'Only my mother. Say, are you sure you aren't using this as an excuse to see what you can dig up? Because if you are, you're going to be very disappointed.'

I got up from the table, clattering the dishes into the sink a bit more energetically than usual. 'What if I am? You are pretty vague about your past, after all. For all I know, there were scores of women before me. Maybe you murdered them one at a time and threw them over the cliff.'

'That isn't funny.' His tone was so sharp that I turned to look at him, but he wasn't watching me. Something had caused him to spill his coffee and he was mopping it up with his napkin.

'The point I'm trying to make,' I said, bringing the dishcloth back to the table, 'is, something made you go out there last night. If we knew what . . . what were you dreaming, anyway?'

'I told you before, I never remember my dreams. I don't even know if I have them.'

Because he still sounded peeved, I hastened to change the subject. 'Well, I think I'll pick up an ankle chain on our next shopping trip, just to be safe. When is our next shopping trip, by the way? I should be making a list.'

'It's Farroday's turn. We alternate, so everybody gets a chance to get away. But I imagine he'll let you ride along with him, if you want.'

'I don't know. He's a bachelor. For all we know, he may have errands of his own that he wouldn't want me along for.'

He grinned as he got my meaning. 'Yes, I guess he might. Tell you what, I'll sort of feel him out on the subject first, all right? If he's planning on sowing any wild oats, you'll have to wait for the next trip.'

The subject was changed. His dreams and his past were forgotten for the moment and he was in his usual good spirits again.

It was not until much later that I was to realize which of my remarks had upset him.

★ ★ ★

After dinner, Alan told me he had to go out for a while.

'I want to check a loose connection on the light,' he explained, 'and I'm going to go over some of the accounts with Farroday.' He hesitated. 'I'm sorry to leave you alone so much.'

'It's all right,' I assured him. 'I can entertain myself, and if I get lonesome, I'll visit your mother.'

I read for a while, and when I checked the time again, I decided it was too late to visit Mrs. Denver. I decided instead I would join Alan and when he finished business, I could walk back with him.

I put on only a light sweater, since I didn't plan on being out in the weather more than a few minutes. Even so, the air was chilly.

I decided to try Farroday's cottage first, but when I approached it, I saw the windows were dark. I retraced my steps and descended the wooden stairs to the lighthouse. By now I was downright cold, and hurrying. The door to the lighthouse stood open, as it often did.

'Alan,' I called, pausing at the bottom of the stairs. There was no reply, but from here the sound of waves on rocks was a roar and if he was up in the tower he might not hear me.

I started up, holding the rail, and felt an odd sense of mounting tension. Since I had set out from the house, I'd had a strange feeling I was being watched, although I had seen no one. I had an urge to look over my shoulder, and restrained myself.

The lighthouse was empty. The light swiveled back on forth on its shiny base. The wind whipped through the open railing, carrying the dampness of the ocean with it. By day the tower had a certain charm, but at night it was eerie and unwelcoming. The wood floors creaked as if invisible feet trod upon them, and the wind created an illusion of whispering voices.

I rubbed my goose-pimpled arms. Alan was not here. Apparently I had missed him on the path. I started rather hurriedly down the winding steps.

I was about halfway down when the door at the bottom slammed shut. The noise was so sudden and so unexpected that I jumped and gave a little cry.

The wind, I thought, banging things around, but I went down the remaining steps even faster than before.

The wind had done more than shove the heavy door shut, however. It had somehow managed to throw the locks as well. The door was shut firmly. I pushed against it, thinking at first that it might only be stuck. It wouldn't budge. I rattled the old brass knob. Nothing happened.

A chill crept up within me. A moment or so earlier, when it had seemed I need be here for no more than a minute or two, I had been able to avoid my feelings of uneasiness. Now, I was not simply uneasy, not even just afraid. I was suddenly terrified of this creaking, howling darkness in which I was trapped.

'Alan,' I cried, banging on the heavy door with my fists, 'Alan, let me out.'

I hurt my fists banging them against the rough wood, and the pain helped bring me back to my senses. Breathing hard, I stepped back and regarded the closed door. It was futile to pound and yell. With all the noise of wind and ocean, my cries would not carry more than a few feet. If Alan were close enough to hear me, he would be on his way to the lighthouse anyway and he would find me without my pounding and screaming.

There wasn't much else that I could do, however, but sit and wait to be found. I sat on the bottom step, but a minute later I jumped back up, too nervous to sit still. I decided I would rather be up at the top. It was open and cold, but at least the light was there and I did not have the sense of being closed in as I did here.

I went back up. The light still swiveled, back and forth, back and forth. I watched it for a minute or so, but it had a hypnotic effect.

If I stood at the railing and leaned out, I could see the lights of our house above. Alan might already be home. He might come looking for me at any minute.

Only, I had told him earlier I might visit his mother. If he did not find me in the house, he would probably think that's where I was.

How long would he wait before he got curious? An hour or so? Surely he would begin to wonder when it got late. He would go to his mother's to fetch me, and when I wasn't there, he'd begin a search. The lighthouse, though, was probably the last place he would think of looking.

It might be morning before chance alone brought anyone here. I shivered at the thought of spending the entire night here. I was already cold under my light sweater. By morning I'd be frozen solid.

I blew on my hands to warm them, and tried walking back and forth. Time dragged by. I looked at my watch after what seemed hours, to discover a mere ten minutes had passed.

My nerves were beginning to fray. I thought I heard footsteps on the stairs and my heart jumped.

'Oh, thank God,' I said aloud, hurrying to the top of the stairs. 'You have no idea how scared I've been.' There was no answer from below.

'Hello,' I called down.

I descended a timid step, and another. It was too dark and too quiet below for comfort. I began to people the darkness with all sorts of dire apparitions. I fancied I heard a faint laugh, though it might have been only the wind.

I had to go down. My throat was dry, my legs unsteady. I went slowly, expecting at each step to see the darkness part before me like a curtain, to find myself face to face with some awful vision.

There was no one. Nothing. At least, I thought grimly, nothing that could be seen. I told myself I could see why people believed in ghosts. I tried to laugh, but unsuccessfully.

I went back up faster than I had come down, but this time the shadows followed me. I stood on the platform above, and every creak of the building was someone creeping up the stairs, every gust of wind a whispered warning.

I looked around frantically for something with which I might force the door open. I was fast losing my self-control. Any minute now I would start to cry and shake and . . .

My eyes fell on the light. Suddenly I remembered something Alan had told me — if the light should go out, a warning bell would alert the keeper.

There must be a switch somewhere to turn the light out, but I saw nothing that looked like one. I stooped down to examine the base. Four screws held a metal plate in place there. I tried one of the screws and found it loose. It turned easily when I used my thumbnail, and the second was not much more of a problem.

The third and fourth ones, however, resisted my efforts. I broke my thumbnail trying. But I remembered I'd put a pin in my hair earlier to hold it back.

My hairpin still wouldn't budge one screw, but it worked on the other, and I was able to move the plate aside, using the one remaining screw as a hinge.

Inside was a maze of wires. Praying that I wasn't about to disconnect the alarm, I took hold of several wires, and yanked.

The light went out in a shower of sparks. At once a warning siren began to howl, high and piercing. I jumped to my feet and ran through the darkness to the stairs, feeling my way down them as fast as I could.

The door opened just as I reached the bottom and Jim Farroday appeared in the opening. I was so relieved that I ran into his arms without thinking.

'Mrs. Denver,' he said, surprised to see me.

'Thank God you're here,' I sobbed, clinging to him.

'What happened to the light? What are you doing in here?'

'I was locked in. I . . . oh, Alan.'

Alan appeared on the path, running toward us. I broke free of Farroday's comforting embrace and ran to my husband.

'What's going on here?' Alan demanded.

'I came to find you,' I sobbed. 'The

door slammed shut and locked. I couldn't get out. I broke the light to tell you where I was.'

He let me cry for a moment. Over my shoulder, he said to Farroday, 'Better fix the light.'

'Sure,' Farroday said. 'Only . . . ' He hesitated.

'What?' Alan asked.

'She said the door was locked, but it was unlocked when I got here.'

I whirled about, astonished. 'But it couldn't be. I tried it. I pounded on it.'

He took hold of the door and opened and closed it. It offered no resistance. I saw what I had not noticed before, a big wooden bolt on the outside of the door.

'The bolt must have fallen.'

'And back up? Besides, it works pretty hard. Try it for yourself.'

I did. The bolt came down, but reluctantly. It was hard to imagine it could have just fallen when the door slammed, and even if it had, how on earth had it gotten back up before Farroday arrived.

'But it was locked,' I said. 'I know it was.'

'It must have stuck,' Alan said. He slammed the door hard twice. It opened with no indication of sticking.

I couldn't begin to guess what had happened. I knew the door had refused to open for me. Something had held it closed. Something, or someone?

'We'd better fix that light,' Alan said. 'Can you get back to the house by yourself?'

'Of course,' I said, a bit coolly, because I knew they did not believe me. 'I'm really not incompetent.'

I started angrily back for the house, but as I walked, my anger became fear again. What had kept me in the lighthouse? And why?

* * *

So many other things had occupied my attention, I had nearly forgotten my own curiosity over the upstairs room that was locked. I was reminded of it later when Mrs. Scruggs came to do her cleaning.

'I seemed to be missing a key to one of the rooms,' I said to her. 'I wonder if I

101

could trouble you to unlock it for me?'

'Which room is that?' she asked. She was in the act of donning a large apron, ruffled in a pretty but unbecoming manner.

I told her. She looked a little surprised. 'No, ma'am,' she said giving her head a shake. 'I can't unlock that one for you.'

'But why on earth not?' I asked, surprised. It had never crossed my mind there would be any difficulty.

'Because I don't have a key to it, that's why,' she replied in a manner that made me think this was a source of some displeasure to her.

'I thought you had keys to everything here,' I said, feeling disappointed.

'I do, everything but that room. It was locked when I came and it's been locked ever since.'

'Maybe one of the keys you do have . . . ' I suggested hesitantly.

She was emphatic. I suppose probably she was as curious as I had been, and as disappointed. 'I tried them all, honey,' she said. 'Every last one. No, ma'am, I never had a key to that door. I asked Mr.

Denver about it too, and he said he didn't know anything about it, and to ask his mother, but she said to let it go, since the room wasn't needed anyway.'

I thought for a moment, digesting this information. She was watching me, an old curiosity clearly whetted once more, to be shared now, hopefully, with another female. I thought perhaps I was mistaken to encourage that sort of intimacy with anyone as a gossipy as Mrs. Scruggs, and I said, 'Well, Mrs. Denver was right, of course. We don't need the room, and it's silly to bother with it. Let's do as she said, and just let it go.'

'Whatever you say.' She looked and sounded a bit let down. 'It's none of my business, I guess, and if you don't think it's yours . . . ' She let that bait dangle briefly, to see if I would snap at it.

'It just doesn't seem important enough to worry about.' I launched quickly into a discussion of the various chores that I thought most needed doing. I had plenty of time on my hands during the week to do housework and had decided it would be more practical to handle the lighter work myself, and save the bigger jobs for her visit, if she didn't mind. We agreed to that plan and when I left her she was busy scrubbing the kitchen floor, a job I was only too happy to leave for her.

Although I had ended our conversation regarding the locked door, however, that did not end my own curiosity. On the contrary, I now found myself more than ever fascinated by it. I could not go along the upstairs hall without wondering about it. Worse, I caught myself once or twice actually going to look at the door, as if by willing it to, I could induce it to speak and tell me what lay beyond. I even stooped down and put my eye to the keyhole. I could see the corner of a bed and part of an old dresser, but nothing more. It looked from the little I could see exactly what it was reported to be — an extra bedroom for which we had no real use.

Now, however, piqued by curiosity, my mind began to supply me with dozens of uses to which that extra room could be put. I had in mind that I would do some sewing, an old pastime of mine, a pleasant and useful way of passing many hours. I needed a place set apart for my work, and it seemed to me now, after several other ideas had come and gone, that the extra bedroom would be an ideal place for my sewing.

The more I thought about this, the more crucial it began to seem to my happiness. I fairly itched to get into that room, not, as I told myself repeatedly, because I thought I would find anything important or interesting in there, but because I now had a real need for it.

I broached the subject with Alan, but with no great success. 'I think the light in there would be perfect,' I said, in the way of making him see how important this was.

'Why don't you use the nursery,' he suggested. He was reading and did not trouble to look up from his book. 'The light in there is excellent. My mother used to paint in there when I was no longer using the room. Has she ever shown you any of her paintings, by the way?'

'No. She never mentioned them.' I might have added that his mother volunteered very little information to me.

Nearly as little as he himself volunteered. I said, 'I'll have to ask her about them.'

So he had succeeded in changing the subject, and I did not know for certain if that had been his intention, but I let it lie.

The next day, I went to pay a call on his mother. I no longer attempted the cliff route, which made me uneasy despite any arguments I could offer myself, and went instead by the longer road. I did not mind the walk, on a nice day, and I had more than enough time to spare.

She greeted me with the proper but unenthusiastic politeness I had come to accept as my due. I had stopped along the way to pick some wildflowers, a pretty blue plant I had no name for, and I gave her these as a gift.

'I'll put them in water,' she said, going into her neat little kitchen. Her house was smaller than ours, truly a cottage, built so that every room looked out over the sea, although the view here was a little less spectacular than where I lived.

There was a smallish living room, with open beams and the inevitable fireplace. On one side of this was a bedroom, and on the other the kitchen and dining area. The entire house was furnished in a comfortable, homey way, with chintz and ruffles I thought rather too fussy for her, although I would not have said so.

She got a container down from a cupboard, and filled it with water.

'Alan says you paint,' I said, trying to find a friendly ground for conversation.

'A little. Not awfully well, I'm afraid.'

'I'd love to see something.'

'That oil in the dining area is the only thing I have up,' she said, busying herself with the flowers.

I had seen that painting before and had noticed nothing unusual about it. It was a seascape, not unlike those at the point, with jagged rocks and the steep cliffs.

Something peculiar happened, though, as I turned to glance at it. Before, studying it, I had seen the superficial scene. Now, looking at it quickly, without preparation, as it were, I saw a different picture altogether.

It was not a sea cliff at all, but a black, rough creature of almost indescribable ugliness and horror. The sharp rocks were not rocks at all, but the teeth of his yawning mouth, waiting to devour his prey. The foaming waves were hands reaching out to seize the unwary.

It filled me with revulsion. I had never looked upon anything so grotesque, so ugly, and I gasped aloud and turned away.

'You don't seem very pleased with it,' she said. She had been watching me, of course. I felt horribly embarrassed. Worse, I felt as if she knew exactly what had caused my reaction.

'I . . . It reminded me of something,' I stammered. I looked again, but this time my eye was ready for it, and I saw only a seascape, once again a picture of cliffs and rocks and the ocean. I could see the lines that had created the other impression, but they did not produce the same effect. It was as if one has seen a face in the clouds, and having looked away, looks back, to decide after all they looked like nothing but clouds.

Nonetheless I was shaken by the incident, the more so because I had a vague impression that Mrs. Denver was amused by my discomfort.

Not that she showed this openly. Instead, she dismissed the painting as of no consequence whatever. 'A silly thing,' she said. 'Shallow, I'm afraid. I have a good technique, but no feeling for what I paint. That's what my instructor in school used to tell me. Let's go into the living room, shall we? I have some fresh lemonade; will you have a glass with me?'

I felt ill at ease during the visit. On the walk over, I had planned how most tactfully to approach the subject of the locked room. I was sure she would know where to find a key, but I was less sure of her willingness to tell me. Now, in the wake of that unfortunate business with the painting, I was shy of broaching the subject, and when I did, shortly before leaving, I did so abruptly, making it all too clear that it had been on my mind the whole time.

'I can't find the key to the bedroom in the wing opposite the nursery,' I said, apropos of nothing we had thus far discussed. 'Do you know where it is?'

'No,' she said. Then, because I must have looked disappointed, she said, 'It can hardly be important, can it? Surely you don't need the room.'

'I wanted to make it into a sewing room.' I realized how trivial and petulant I sounded, and it only made me feel all the more defensive. 'I don't understand why the room is locked in the first place.'

'I don't understand why it should be so important to you.' Something in her tone was so like my own petulance, that I suddenly realized it was as important to her that the room remained locked as it was for me to see it opened.

'What is in that room?' I asked boldly. Her eyes flashed angrily, warning me away from the subject, but I met the challenge without flinching. I wanted to be friends with this woman and I was willing to be merely polite, if she preferred that, but I did not intend to be cowed by her.

'Nothing,' she said, far too sharply.

We stood for a moment in silence. Then, as we were already at the door, I turned to leave. 'Well,' I said, 'there are ways to open locked doors, without keys.'

I let myself out, and started along the walk that led to the road.

'Karen,' she called after me. When I looked back, she had regained the cool poise I faintly envied her for. She looked regal and strong. I thought she would be a dangerous enemy.

'Perhaps locked doors are safest left locked,' she said. 'If they were locked for a reason.'

It was an admission that I was right, that something was hidden in that locked room. I was so pleased with this confirmation of my suspicions that I failed to heed the warning she had given me.

'Perhaps they are best unlocked, if unlocked for a reason.'

'Some secrets are best left to lie. Leave the ghosts of the past to their graves.'

'But they haven't stayed in them, have they? Perhaps they too want that room opened. Perhaps that's why they've haunted the Point.'

I left, walking quickly and angrily in the direction of home. I no longer tried to deceive myself that I had an important use for that room. Frankly and simply, I wanted to see what was in there.

And I meant to do so at once.

5

I did not, after all, have the opportunity to satisfy my curiosity that same day. Alan was in the house when I came in on my return. In my anger and determination, I had walked the entire distance at a fast clip. I was sweaty and my blonde hair had been blown by the wind so that it hung in disarray about my face.

'Hi,' Alan greeted me and then, getting a better look at me, he asked, 'Is something wrong?'

'Only that I've been quarreling with your mother,' I said impulsively.

'What on earth about?' he asked, genuinely surprised.

'That locked room upstairs,' I said.

'That room?' He looked all the more surprised and then broke into laughter. 'Of all the silly things to quarrel about.'

'I'm sorry, but I don't find it amusing,' I said coolly.

Seeing the expression on my face, he

stopped laughing, but he was not at all sympathetic to my point of view. Rather, he became suddenly angry with me.

'Look,' he said, speaking more sharply than I would have thought the discussion warranted. 'You've got some sort of bee in your bonnet about that room. I think you ought to forget about it.'

'I can't just forget it,' I said.

'Blast it, you can,' he snapped. 'Put it out of your head. It's locked. Leave it at that. You can't do any good by poking and prying into things that don't concern you.'

I was so surprised by his remarks and by his angry manner that I could not think of what to say to argue the point further.

Apparently he took my silence as acquiescence. He gave me a brief kiss, no longer angry, but not exactly affectionate either, and went out.

I did not intend, however, to leave the matter at that. His attitude sounded so like that of his mother that I could not help feeling that Alan, too, knew there was something in the room, something deliberately hidden and locked away from me. If this was so, then he had kept that fact concealed from me when I had asked about the room before, and that was dishonest, whether or not he had actually lied to me about it.

I was certain now that something was being kept from me, some secret shared by Alan and his mother. I was determined to learn what it was.

I was determined, too, to see into that locked room, but I had seen that the subject for some reason provoked Alan's anger. To pursue it further just now would almost certainly result in a quarrel.

I decided it was best to let the matter rest for a day or two, until I could find some discreet way of solving the problem. Alan had not flatly forbidden me to go into the room, however close he had come to that.

I had an idea what I would do, when the right time came.

It was Mrs. Scruggs' cleaning day again when the right opportunity presented itself. Soon after the jovial housekeeper had arrived, Alan told me he was going to have to take the pickup truck and drive into Santa Barbara. Some part, I couldn't begin to understand what, needed replacing in the light system, and Santa Barbara, some forty miles away, was the nearest place he could get it.

I waited a decent interval after he was gone, in the hope that Mrs. Scruggs would not connect in her mind his departure with my request. Then I sought her out, in the dining room, where she had just finished waxing the floor.

'I haven't been able to find the key to that locked room,' I said, pretending I didn't see the look of pleasant anticipation that came across her face at once. 'Tell me, if you couldn't find a key and wanted to get into a room, what would you do? Pick a lock?'

'Why, Ma'am, nothing could be simpler,' she said, putting aside the sponge mop she had been using. 'All you have to do is remove the door from the hinges.'

'Is it difficult?'

She had been waiting for that question. 'You just come with me,' she said, leading the way to the kitchen, 'and we'll have that room open in a jiffy.'

From the kitchen, she armed herself with a meat cleaver, a screwdriver, and a small hammer that we kept in the tool drawer there. She led the way up the stairs, hurrying as if she were afraid I might at any moment change my mind and deprive her of her triumph.

I got the impression she had been through this ritual before. Locked doors represented little challenge to Mrs. Scruggs. She drove the blade of the cleaver between the hinge and the head of the bolt that passed through the hinge, using the hammer to drive it in.

When she had edged the bolt up a bit, she replaced the cleaver with the screwdriver. A few good taps on the handle of the screwdriver drove the bolt up to where it could simply be lifted out by hand. The second hinge got the same treatment, and she had only to lift the door off its hinges, and set it aside, and the locked room was open.

At first glance, it was disappointing. Not that it was not a lovely room. It was a charming one. It was a bedroom, as I had already known, and had evidently belonged to, or been decorated by, a woman, with lace and chintz and pretty pastel colors, and a profusion of bows and frills. The room had a little-girl quality about it that was sweet almost to the point of being cloying.

I found no bodies lying about draped in black, however, nor equipment for torture, nor men in iron masks.

I really did not know what I had been expecting. I suppose my imagination had been content to convince me that I would find something stupendous, but I found myself in what was after all rather an ordinary bedroom, and I could not but feel a bit disappointed.

'Why, look at this, would you?' Mrs. Scruggs said. She too had been surveying the room and looking a trifle disappointed, but regarding everything with a keen eye that was determined to find anything of interest here.

So, she was the first to see the dress, lying at one corner of the bed, and she went to it without a thought of asking my permission. We were in this together now, she and I, and she made it plain that she knew it.

'It's rose point,' she said, fingering the lace. She held back at the stage of picking the dress up. She was, after all, the cleaning lady.

I had no such reservations. I went to where she was standing and picked up the dress from the bed. It was a gown, vaguely old-fashioned looking, and long. It was of lace, incredibly lovely lace of a cream color, and very finely done. Even with my untrained eye, I could see that.

'Rose point?' I asked, fingering the delicate looking cloth in my hand.

'That's what this style of lace is called,' she explained. She took a closer look. 'Oh,' she exclaimed, 'Look at that, would you.'

I looked where she pointed. I had only been studying a piece of the cloth, and not observing the gown as a whole. Now I saw what had caused her exclamation. The dress, which had once been very lovely, was torn badly in several places, the lace hanging in tattered shreds. It had been lying on the bed so that the tears were not apparent. Hanging from my arm as it was now, it was obvious that the gown had been quite ruined.

There were several bad stains on the gown too, of a brownish hue. I brought one up to the light to examine it more closely.

'Why, that's blood, isn't it?' Mrs. Scruggs said, peering intently over my shoulder.

'Is it? It's hard to say,' I said, but I thought she was probably right.

Someone had worn this dress in the past. Had worn it, and had been in some sort of accident that had caused tears and bloodstains. The woman wearing it had been badly hurt, perhaps even killed.

Someone else, surely, had left the gown in this room and locked the door, and put the key I knew not where. Locked the door and hidden the key so that the gown would be hidden, and I would not see it.

Whose gown was it, I wondered? Who had worn it in that fateful past, and suffered those cuts and tears? What had happened to her?

And why had the gown been hidden

behind a locked door?

The dress was not alone — there was a veil, too, on the bed.

I picked up the veil, fingering the fine pattern. It was not difficult to see from where the design had gotten its name. It was a pattern of roses, as gossamer and fragile as if born of mist.

Mrs. Scruggs had been standing in contemplative silence watching my interest in the gown and its veil. I knew her mind was trying to sort out the various facts and impressions, putting them into a better order for the telling later.

I could only hope it looked clearer to her than it did to me. The pattern of what had happened since I had come here was as airy and delicate as this lace, but in the fabric, I could trace the pattern, and in life I could not yet discern it, although I knew that a pattern existed.

'If you're wanting to know about the lace,' Mrs. Scruggs said, breaking the silence that had descended between us, 'you ought to go to Mrs. Myers at the library in Lompoc. That's how I know this is rose point. She collects it and has all kinds of books on the subject. It's fascinating, really, to hear her talk about it.'

I stood for a moment more in indecision. I wanted to know about it now, about the real persons who had touched this damaged lace, but Alan was gone, and he was the one, I felt certain, who could give me the answers I wanted.

The gauzy fabric in my hands fascinated me, though. I could not help but think of the dreams that had accompanied it, of the loves it had known. It was old, and I thought that if it could only speak to me, it could tell me of many of the mysteries of life.

I decided I would drive into Lompoc. Alan had taken the truck, leaving the car behind, and Mrs. Scruggs would be here should anything come up at the house. I knew full well that she would like to be going with me, adding other pieces to the puzzle she would soon enough share with friends and neighbors.

I left her to her cleaning, however, and with instructions from her on where to find Mrs. Myers, I drove into Lompoc. I took the veil with me to show the librarian. The dress itself I moved to my room, and the door we replaced on its hinges, after fixing the lock so that now it would open.

The library was a charming, old Spanish-style building on a quiet, shady street. It was cool inside. This, and the sense of timelessness, calmed me a little. I found Mrs. Myers. Like the building itself, she seemed to me an anachronism.

I told her who I was, and that Mrs. Scruggs had sent me to her.

'Yes, Eleanor has spoken of you often, and highly,' she said. 'Oh, how lovely.'

I had unfolded the lace veil from my purse, and handed it across the desk to her. She took it carefully, as if afraid it might disintegrate at her touch.

'*Point de gaze*,' she said in a whisper, not looking at me but at the exquisite needlework. 'Rose point, they call it. It's a type of Chantilly lace, but blonde, not dark like the true Chantilly. It's silk. Nineteenth century, I should say. Rose point was the most popular lace then. There was an aura, almost of mystery, about it — few knew how to create it, and the nuns who did so kept everything about it secret, even to what threads they used. Of course, in time the art of it passed away with those who knew it. It's very rare today, especially such a beautiful example as this.'

She did look up at me finally, but reluctantly. I had the feeling Mrs. Myers preferred her laces to people, but she made an effort to be interested in me.

'Is it yours?' she asked.

'Not exactly,' I replied. 'I found it at the house. I wondered if it were valuable?'

'Oh, yes, very,' she said, her head bobbing. 'I have a picture of a veil here — wait.' She went to a bookcase, selected a book thoughtfully, and thumbed quickly through it. She found what she was seeking and brought it to me. It was a photograph of a veil, not unlike the one I had brought with me.

'Cornelia Vanderbilt wore this in eighteen eighty-nine when she married Baron Clemens Freiher von Zedlitz. It's worth, I should say, about ten thousand dollars.'

'I had no idea lace was so precious,' I said, truly surprised. I turned the pages lightly. There were other photographs, with captions giving the names of the laces. They were redolent of the past, of a more gracious way of life than what we knew today — point d'Angleterre, Rosaline, Mechlin, which the author called the Queen of Laces.

'Oh, yes,' she said, pleased that she had been able to impress me. 'This piece is not that precious, of course, but any lace, real lace, is quite valuable. It's finished, you see. Not just rose point, but all the really great lace we'll ever have, we have already. Handmade lace is a thing of the past, a lost art, almost. Its legacy is measured in those cobwebs of cloth.'

'Isn't it being made anymore?' I asked. I had somehow just supposed that lace was ever available.

'Not like that, by hand,' she said. 'Just think, a really diligent worker might be able in, say, three week's time, to produce an inch of that. Even the threads used in the great laces are virtually gone. I know of skeins that are kept in locked vaults, in the event a repair is needed.'

I had turned to yet another photograph of a particularly elaborate lace veil. I paused, studying it with new appreciation of what it represented.

'That,' Mrs. Myers said, beaming with all the pride of a new parent, 'is the veil worn by the Archduchess Marie Louise of Austria when she married Napoleon. If you look carefully, you will see all the emblems of empire — the imperial bees and eagle, the crown imperial lily, even Marie's own initial.

'To know lace is to know the history of romance. Empress Eugenie adored wild flowers. Napoleon III first saw her running barefoot on a beach with wild flowers in her hair. So her wedding veil was of Alençon lace, strewn with wild flowers in colored silk. Brides in those days, wanted, as the expression has it, 'a wreath that does not fade of flowers that blow.''

She talked on, eager for someone willing to listen, and it was, as she had said, a history of romance. The threads of her story spun from the ancient tombs of Egypt to the temples of Peru and China, around the world and through the centuries. She conjured dandies and royal figures, like the men of the Petit Trianon who, while their ladies made a game of farming, took to making lace and carried their gold lace-making tools about in little purses called reticules. Magical phrases abounded — stitches such as 'sown with tears,' mignonette, 'toad in the hole,' fountain of marriage,' and 'holy virgins.'

'Even the beginnings of lace making are shrouded in mystery,' she said. 'According to legend, Flemish lace-making began with a miracle. A young girl at Bruges was working one day under a tree with her needle and thread. Her mother was dying and the girl had no money. She prayed for a way to support her mother, and a perfectly formed spider web fell into her apron. She tried to copy the web with her needle, but the threads tangled. Her lover suggested she tie each thread to a separate twig and weave them back and forth. She did, and bobbin lace making was begun.'

She took the book from me, closing it

sadly, almost reverentially. 'Lace became so popular in the nineteenth century that machine-made lace was created, and eventually, because it was cheaper, it replaced the handmade variety. To be sure, there were purists who held to the old standards for a time. Florence Nightingale put it categorically: 'no gentlewoman ever wears anything but real lace.' But the art was finished. Today a few collectors have most of the really good lace.'

She picked up the veil I had brought with me and handed it lovingly back to me. The gesture spoke more eloquently than words of her feeling for the lace.

'This,' she said, 'was some fortunate young woman's bridal veil. It's difficult to imagine its being put away somewhere and neglected. I'm sure that whoever the bride was, when she wore this, dreamed of someday handing it down to her daughter, as it must have been handed down to her by her mother, and perhaps her mother's mother before that. It's quite old.'

Her words gave me a start. I had not

thought of the gown and the veil in this light before, but when I looked down at the cloth in my hands, I saw at once that she was right. It was a bridal veil, of course. I should have seen that for myself when I looked at the gown. Seeing it now in my mind, it was clear that it had been a wedding gown.

I saw too the dreadful stains and tears in the cloth. The dreamy loveliness of that wedding had dissolved into a nightmare for the young woman who had worn the bridal gown of rose point lace. And she had left her precious heirloom not for her daughter to wear, but for me to find it and be frightened by it.

Who had she been, that lace-gowned bride? And who had been the groom, the man whose hand had held hers as Alan's had held mine a short time before, while they heard the same words that had been spoken over Alan and me?

★   ★   ★

I left soon after, thanking Mrs. Myers for the time she had given me.

128

'Don't thank me,' she said, squeezing my hand warmly. 'You have no idea what a pleasure it is for me to talk of these things with someone. So few people have any interest in them anymore.'

I did not want to disappoint her by telling her the reasons for my interest, although I felt confident she would soon enough hear some details from Mrs. Scruggs, directly or indirectly.

On the drive home I let my thoughts sift through the web of information she had given me. I had learned a great deal about lace, but unfortunately the things I really wanted to know were still mysteries.

Looking back over the period of time since I had come to the Point as a new bride, I could begin to see a pattern emerging that was disquieting. I thought of Alan's vagueness regarding his past, a vagueness that seemed genuine, yet too complete. Did he genuinely not remember anything, or was he deliberately holding things back from me?

I thought, too, of that woman in the shop in Lompoc who had referred to the other Mrs. Denver, and to some tragic incident that had occurred.

Tragic. And the gown of rose point lace was torn and blood-stained, and then locked away so no one would see it. Where I was deliberately discouraged from discovering it.

The clues all pointed to one conclusion, but it was one I did not want to face. Had Alan lied to me? Had there been another Mrs. Denver, another bride? Had he married before and not only not told me of it, but lied when I questioned him?

The idea rankled, but how else could I explain everything that had happened?

If there had been a bride before me, who had worn a wedding gown of rose point lace, what had become of her? Something tragic, clearly, something that tore cloth and left stains, that would seem obvious. And that left no one behind.

I remembered then the hand that had tapped at night at the window, seeming to summon me outside. Surely that had been real, and not the hand of a ghost. Had it been the hand of another Mrs. Denver — of Emily?

I was torn by these thoughts. One part of me reminded me of how desperately I loved my husband, and warned me that I must trust and believe in him if our marriage was to survive. This voice, however, was less insistent than the one that told me I must face the facts squarely, and only then could I hope to deal with them and extricate myself and Alan from a web of intrigue that seemed to be drawing tighter about us.

The road turned, and in the distance I saw the house that was now my home. I had seen it first in the rain and darkness, yet it had seemed to me then comforting and romantic and lovely. It was a paradox that now, by bright sunlight, it looked grim and forbidding to me.

I felt the presence of danger within those gray walls, a danger of some nameless sort that hovered always nearby. I thought of Mother Denver's ghosts. Yes, this place was indeed haunted, haunted by its past. One need not believe in wandering spirits to believe that. I was threatened as surely as if some headless horror roamed the halls.

And this seemed to me all the more ominous because I could not put a name or a face to the dangers that threatened me. I knew they were there, but not what they were. It was like the murmur of voices in another room. One knows that someone is speaking, but one cannot tell what is being said.

I entered the house and, seeing Mrs. Scruggs, made an effort to shake off these gloomy thoughts. If nothing else, I owed it to Alan to keep these difficulties private, until I better understood them.

Mrs. Scruggs looked all eager anticipation. 'Did you find Mrs. Myers all right?' She asked.

'Yes, thank you,' I said, putting the lace carefully into a closet where it would not be conspicuous. 'Your directions were perfect.'

She waited in scarcely contained excitement. I knew that I would have to tell her something, however trivial, if I was to have any peace at all.

'She was most helpful,' I said. 'She told me a great deal of the history of lace making. I had no idea it was such a fascinating subject.'

'Could she tell you anything about that piece you took with you?' Mrs. Scruggs asked.

'Oh, yes. She said it was rose point, as you thought. *Point de gaze*, she called it. An old piece, probably rather valuable.' I did not add that it was much too valuable for anyone simply to forget that it existed, leaving it to lie neglected in a locked room.

It was a disappointing answer, of course, because it answered only the question she had asked, and not the one that was simply understood, but she could hardly pursue it further since I seemed reluctant to do so.

'I see,' she said flatly, and when I made it plain that I did not mean to volunteer any more information, she went back to her housework. I had no doubt that she felt cheated, having given her aid freely in getting into the room, only to be frustrated in the gossip she had hoped to gather. When she had finished her work, and was preparing to leave, she was definitely subdued and cool. I pretended not to notice, and after making as slow a process as she could out of getting ready to leave, she did so, and I was at last alone.

I was not really alone though. My thoughts remained with me, buzzing about my head like so many flies, and just as troublesome. My head ached from trying to answer the questions in my mind, and still no answers came.

It was evening before Alan arrived home. I had managed to busy myself in preparing dinner, and that had helped to take my mind off the other matters, but Alan's presence brought it all painfully back to me.

'Traffic was murder coming out of Santa Barbara,' he said, kissing me. 'Sorry I'm late. Do I have time for a drink?'

I told him he had. 'There's something I want to talk to you about,' I added.

'Sure,' he said, fixing himself a drink.

'Wait,' I said. 'I'll be right back.'

This time I wanted no vague replies. I wanted the lace gown in my hand, something real that had to be explained, not an impression that might be nothing more than fancy. I left him looking curious but amused, and ran up the steps. The gown was in our room, but out of the way in the closet. I took it out, holding it for a moment in my hands, staring at the tears and the stains.

I knew I was risking a quarrel. Alan had not exactly ordered me to forget the locked room in which the gown had been hidden, but he had certainly come close to that.

And there was certainly some reason why this dress had been locked away there in the first place. If he had wanted me to know of it, and whatever story was linked with it, he would have long ago told me of it, or at the very least, given me answers to my questions when I asked him.

I could, of course, choose to put the dress back where I had found it, lock the door once again, and let the matter lie, as he and his mother so obviously both wanted me to do.

I was tempted. I did not look forward to the prospect of a quarrel with my husband. And I was afraid of what I might learn.

It was no use, though. It was too late to pretend I did not know of the dress, or that the questions had not already been asked, if only in my mind. And I knew I would have no peace until I asked them aloud, and they had been answered. They were like a sore that must be lanced, although it would hurt a little, to prevent a far greater infection from developing.

Holding the dress carefully in my arms, mindful now of its value, I came down the stairs to the living room where Alan waited.

He had gone to the window to look out at the sea. The sun was setting, and the sky and the distant ocean were a dusty rose hue. From here the sea looked calm and peaceful, and one could almost forget the turbulent waves and the violent currents beneath the placid surface.

He heard me come into the room, and turned from the window. His smile froze on his lips, and his eyes grew wide. I do not know how better to describe the expression on his face than to say that it was one of horror. He tried to speak, but no words would come from his mouth.

The glass in his hand slipped from his fingers and fell to the floor with a crash, sending glass and whisky across the carpet.

He put a hand to his throat, as if he were strangling, and I was frightened half out of my wits by this unexpectedly violent reaction to the sight of me, and the gown in my hands.

'Alan,' I cried, taking a small step forward. 'What is it, for heaven's sake?'

My heart pounded. I couldn't imagine what I had done wrong, but I knew I had handled this badly. Whatever memories the dress held for him, they were horrible indeed. I had opened the door on some dread monsters of his past, and I knew not how to close it again.

He tried once more to speak, but nothing came out except a hoarse cry.

Suddenly he sprang forward. I thought for a moment that he meant to seize me, and instinctively I stepped aside.

Instead, however, he ran past me, almost knocking me aside. There was something of the demon in that headlong flight of his. He ran down the hall like a man possessed and, terrified, I ran after him.

'Alan,' I called. The door at the rear of the house slammed open. By the time I reached it, he was already racing across the distance that separated the house from the cliff, running toward the cliff.

I knew he meant to throw himself over and I could do nothing to stop him. A scream of horror escaped my lips.

It was my scream, futile as it seemed, that saved him after all. He faltered, stumbling, as if it had recalled him to his senses and broken the spell that was driving him to his doom.

He staggered, no longer running headlong for the edge, and finally sank to his knees. He seemed to crumple, as if all the life had fled his body, and he sank to the ground in a heap.

'Darling,' I sobbed, running to him, but he was beyond hearing. He was unconscious. For one horrible moment I thought he had died, that the horror he had experienced had been more than a human heart could bear — but he had only fainted under the weight of his burden.

I tried to rouse him, but I couldn't.

Nor could I even hope to get him inside by myself. Evening was falling. I had no idea of the nature of the coma into which he had fallen, nor how long it would last. I could hardly leave him here, nor trust his behavior should he awaken by himself, perhaps still driven by the same nightmare that had carried him almost to the cliff's edge.

I needed help and, jumping up, I ran as fast as I could to the nearest place where I could find it.

'Mr. Farroday, Mr. Farroday,' I cried, pounding my fists on the door of the little cottage in which the other lighthouse keeper lived.

He answered my frantic pounding at once, looking startled by the intrusion. 'Mrs. Denver. What's wrong?'

'Alan,' I gasped, literally out of breath. 'I . . . please, come.' I grabbed his arm, practically yanking him out the door.

To his credit, he put aside any further questions, no doubt seeing that I was hardly in condition to answer them, and instead he came with me up the path, covering the distance with one long stride for every two of mine.

He saw Alan before we reached him and broke into a run, easily outdistancing me. By the time I reached them, Farroday was down on his knees looking Alan over.

'What happened?' he demanded of me as I ran up. 'Has he been hurt?'

'No, he fainted,' I said.

His eyebrows went up at that. I knew the sort of thoughts he was thinking. Alan was not the frail and wan type of man, the fainting type. He was strong and healthy and quite manly. I knew Farroday was wondering what could have caused a man of Alan's robust constitution to sink into unconsciousness like this.

'Please,' I said, still short of breath. 'I'll try to explain, but first help me get him inside, will you?'

He put his questions aside for later and did as I asked without further comment. He was a strong man, and although one could easily see that Alan was no featherweight, Farroday was able to lift him and throw him over his shoulder.

'Get the door,' he said, starting off for the house.

I ran ahead, opening doors, leading the way up to the bedroom. There, with Farroday's help, I got my husband undressed and into bed. It was all I could do, short of calling for an ambulance, and I felt instinctively Alan would not want that.

I knew his unconsciousness was a kind of mental escape, for which I doubt there was any physical relief. My only hope was that sleep would relieve the nightmare that had nearly taken his life.

Farroday came back downstairs with me. I saw that he was waiting for an explanation, and I truly felt that I owed him one. Only, it was difficult to explain to someone else what I myself did not understand.

'Would you like a drink?' I asked, leading the way into the living room. The broken glass that Alan had dropped still lay on the floor with a pool of whiskey slowly drying about it. Near the door lay the gown of rose point lace where I had dropped it when I had gone in pursuit of Alan. I saw Farroday's quick eyes take in all these things, but he waited tactfully for me to explain.

'I wouldn't mind some whisky,' he said.

I poured him some in a glass. When I handed it to him I managed a wan smile and said, 'I suppose you're wondering what that was all about?'

'I am, a little,' he said with a grin. 'I find your husband passed out on the grass and you running around banging on doors and looking like the devil himself was after you.'

'He was, I think,' I said ruefully. 'The trouble is, I don't know much myself, not everything certainly, but I'll tell you what I know. I found a dress, that dress there, in a locked room upstairs. I showed it to Alan and he went into a panic. He ran from the house, I think he would have thrown himself over the cliff, except that I screamed. That seemed to make him stumble. He fainted, and when I couldn't rouse him, I came after you.'

He took a swallow of the whisky, studying me over the rim of the glass as if he had not quite made up his mind to believe me. I could well understand his uncertainty.

'I know it doesn't make much sense,' I said. 'Believe me, it doesn't to me either.'

'It's a little hard to understand,' he agreed. He relaxed a bit. I thought he had made up his mind more or less in my favor, although he still regarded the matter as highly curious.

'Oh, there's more to it, of course,' I said. 'But I don't understand any of it either. Maybe you do. What went on here in this house before I came?'

'Nothing of any particular interest,' he said, meeting my questioning gaze frankly. 'Things are always quiet here — quieter before you came than they are now, to be honest.'

He did not say that as if he were criticizing me, but I knew what he meant. He must have heard about my own near accident on the cliffs and he certainly knew of the confusion when I was trapped in the lighthouse. Probably he knew of Alan's sleepwalking incident as well — and now this.

'But there must have been something,' I said. 'It seems to have been something

143

involving a woman. A woman named Emily.'

He pursed his lips, regarding me. I knew he was thinking the sort of things a man thinks about another man and a woman. No doubt he was wondering whether for Alan's sake he ought to dodge this question altogether.

He said, 'You know, I have no business discussing that sort of thing with you so far as your husband's activities are concerned. Especially his past activities. He's a normal, healthy man, if you get my point.'

'Oh, I'm not just being a prying female,' I said impatiently. 'You must see how important this is.'

He relented a little. 'I can tell you this much, I don't remember ever hearing the name Emily,' he said. 'And if you're asking was there some other woman living here, the answer is no. That is, not since I came, but I've been here just a little less than a year, so I can't answer for what might have gone on before that.'

'I didn't know you had been here so short a time,' I said, thinking over this piece of information, turning it about in my mind to see where, if at all, it fit into my puzzle. 'Who was here before you came?' I asked.

'I have no idea. Alan never talked about him. To be honest, I got the impression he didn't want to, so I never asked much. I had no reason to, you understand. It was nothing to me why my predecessor came or went.' He paused, reflecting, and I could see he was truly searching his memory for anything that might be useful.

'He left in a hurry, though,' he said. 'A lot of his things were still here when I came. I asked your husband what to do about them but he was pretty vague. His mother came by one day, and said he'd left kind of sudden like, and she doubted that he would be coming back for anything. So I packed up everything that was his in some boxes and we put them in the storeroom. They're still there, or they were the last I noticed them.'

It fitted with all the rest — a man who left abruptly, Alan's vagueness on the subject, even his mother's apparent taking charge of the situation, but it did nothing to make the picture any clearer.

'Look,' he said, finishing his drink. 'I like your husband. He's a nice guy and I figure I'm a pretty good judge of a man's character. Maybe he has got a secret or two that he doesn't want everybody to know about, but then, so do most men. It's none of my affair, of course, but maybe you ought to let things alone. Maybe you're stirring up a hornet's nest that doesn't need stirring up at all. Have you thought of that?'

I sighed aloud. 'Yes, I have,' I said, 'but in the first place, I'm not everybody, I'm his wife. And in the second place, I didn't stir up this nest, it was already buzzing. And I don't think it's going to stop until I've learned the answers to some questions.'

'What if those answers don't solve the problem?'

'The problem is still there. I think you'd have to agree with me, that there is something seriously out of line with a man who freaks out at the sight of a bit of lace, and tries to kill himself. As his wife,

I have to think there is a solution. And I have to try to find it.'

He shrugged, as much as to remind me that it wasn't his business. 'Well, if you need me again, you give a whistle,' he said.

He went out and I was alone again with my tormenting thoughts.

6

I knew where I could find the answers to my questions. Of course, Alan could undoubtedly answer some of them, but I had in effect asked him by showing him the gown, and the result had been nearly tragic. I did not want to run that risk again unless I had to.

His mother, however, almost certainly knew the meaning to the mystery surrounding me here, if she would only divulge it. I made up my mind that she must, that I would somehow pry the explanation from her.

Had it been possible, I would surely have gone directly to her that night with my demands, but I did not want to risk leaving Alan unattended, and I was reluctant to call on Farroday again to ask him to stay with Alan. In any event, by now it was growing late, and it seemed far more sensible to wait until morning to pursue the matter.

I had a faint hope that Alan might, when he woke and on his own initiative, offer me some explanation for his behavior.

Such was not the case, however. I woke before Alan did in the morning, and went downstairs to make coffee. He woke up when I came back into the bedroom with his morning coffee. He sat up, stretching and grinning in a sleepy fashion.

'Hey, what's this?' he asked when I set the coffee down on the nightstand. 'Breakfast in bed? What's the occasion?'

'I thought after last night you might need it,' I said, watching closely for his reaction. Just now he looked no different than he did any other morning. If he had suffered some great shock the night before, he had come through it with flying colors.

'Last night?' He screwed up his face in an effort to remember. 'What happened last night that was so special?'

I realized that he wasn't being merely evasive. He truly did not remember anything out of the ordinary.

'You don't remember?'

'Should I?' he asked, only looking more puzzled. 'I don't remember very much of last night, as a matter of fact. Let me see. I know I fixed myself a drink before dinner. I was beat from being on the road.'

He laughed aloud. 'Boy, that drink must really have hit me. I hope I wasn't too bad. I don't remember a thing after I had it. No wonder you thought I'd need breakfast in bed this morning.'

He swung his feet to the floor. 'Sorry to disappoint you, though,' he said, getting up and taking a tentative sip from the coffee cup. 'But I don't seem to have much of a hangover, regardless of how much you might think I deserve one.'

It gave me an eerie sensation to think of how close he had come to death, how truly horrified he had been at the sight of that tattered gown the night before, and yet to see how at peace he was this morning.

Something of these thoughts must have shown in my face, because he put an affectionate arm about me. 'Hey, did I act that badly?' he asked. 'You look pretty low.'

I came very close to telling him the truth . . . but I was afraid of the consequences. Instead, I managed a pale smile and said, 'No, you were fine, really. I just slept badly, that's all. I have a slight headache.'

He seemed to accept that. Perhaps some other part of his mind knew the truth, and understood the lie, and wanted him to accept it. At any rate, he did not question me further and the day went on as if it were like any other, and nothing extraordinary had happened between us.

When Alan had gone out to work, I dressed and made ready for a visit to his mother's cottage. I was determined to see her and get the truth out of her. I felt certain if I just told her what had happened, she would come around to my way of thinking. After all, regardless of whether she did or did not resent me, she certainly loved Alan and she would not want to allow anything to continue that threatened not only his happiness, but his life as well.

I had put the rose point gown away before retiring the night before, lest Alan come across it inadvertently and be provoked to a repeat of his behavior. Now I got it down again and, folding it into a neat bundle, I put it into the carryall I sometimes used as a purse. Presented with the gown, Mrs. Denver could hardly deny its existence or that she knew its history.

We had slept late and by now it was already midmorning. I could not make the long walk to Mrs. Denver's house and back in time for lunch, and I knew that Alan expected me to prepare his lunch.

It meant I had to wait, trying to keep myself busy and my mind occupied. The hour before lunch seemed to last forever.

Alan chose this day to be later than usual coming in for lunch, so that I was really quite a bundle of nerves. He could not help but notice.

'Still got that headache?' he asked across the table. I nodded and concentrated on my salad. 'Maybe you ought to take it easy for the rest of the day,' he suggested.

'As a matter of fact, I thought I'd take the afternoon off and stroll over to see your mother. It's been a couple of days since I've seen her.'

'I'm glad you're making the effort to be friends with her,' he said, looking pleased.

When he had gone back to work and I had hastily cleared up the lunch dishes, I set out along the road. It was a lovely day, sunny and pleasantly warm. My oppressed spirits lifted a little as I walked.

An old gentleman in a battered truck that might once have been blue came by. He nearly suffocated me in a cloud of dust and exhaust, coming to a quick stop, and when I had walked alongside the cab of the truck, he leaned out to ask, 'Want a lift, young lady?'

In the city I might have been reluctant, but living as I did far from the city crowds, and thinking this oldster represented no kind of threat, I thanked him and got in, and he started up again. I glanced behind at the fresh cloud of dust he had raised in taking off and was grateful I was inside and not behind the truck.

'It was kind of you to stop and offer a stranger a lift,' I said.

'What's that?' he asked. 'Strangers, us?' He chuckled as if something had struck him as quite amusing. There was a sharp bend in the road ahead and he concentrated on negotiating that. From his manner of driving I had reached the conclusion that he did not see terribly well and I wondered if I was altogether safe riding with him.

After he had made the turn, leaning well forward over the wheel and squinting his eyes till they were mere slits in his wizened face, he said, 'So you think we're strangers, heh? That's a good one.' He chuckled again.

Suddenly I had a premonition of where this conversation was leading. I had an eerie feeling of déjà vu, as if I had been through all this before. I could almost predict each line of our dialogue.

'Have we met before?' I asked. My voice had a tremulous ring to it.

He glanced once at me, squinting again, but I felt he did not see me altogether clearly. I tried to imagine my appearance as it was to him, blurred a little, the general impression there, but not the details.

'I used to see you all the time, didn't I?' he said, looking back at the road, which required most of his limited vision. 'You're the girl from the lighthouse, ain't you?'

'Yes,' I said, and this time my voice barely made it above the noise of the truck.

'And I'll bet you're going to your mother-in-law's place just up the road.'

'Yes,' I said again. He cackled and waited expectantly.

I felt as if I were drowning, in over my head, an urgent current bearing me swiftly, inescapably along, to batter me against the rocks.

'It's been so long since I saw you,' I said, picking my way among the rocks as cautiously as I could.

He was clearly delighted that I had remembered. 'Now that you mention it,' he said, 'it has been a year or more. Used to give you a lift two or even three times a week. Say, how's that young man of yours? What his name? Albert?'

I closed my eyes. The waves rushed over me. I couldn't breathe.

'Alan,' I managed to say. 'He . . . he's just fine, thank you.'

The clatter faded. The rough jiggling about lessened. I thought for a moment I was losing consciousness, but my eyes opened at my command and I saw that we had merely come to a stop.

My companion was squinting at me again, his expression worried. 'You all right there?' he wanted to know.

I swallowed and somehow found the voice to say, 'Yes, I'm fine, thanks.' We sat for a moment more and I suddenly realized why we had stopped. We were at the lane that led down to my mother-in-law's house. I could see the tiled roof in the distance. He had indeed known exactly where I was going. There was no likelihood of any mistake.

I opened the door and got down out of the cab. My legs felt unsteady.

'You been sick?' the old gentleman asked, leaning out of the cab. 'You don't look so hot.'

'I'm all right,' I said. I moved away

from the truck because I thought I could not endure any more of this conversation, or what it was doing to me. 'Thank you again, and goodbye.'

He appeared to be satisfied with that. He put the truck noisily in gear, but as he was pulling away, he called loudly, 'Well, goodbye now, Miss Emily.'

Then he was gone in another cloud of dust.

The lane toward Mrs. Denver's cottage stretched before me, but I could not go down it at once. I had to have time first to collect my scattered wits, and calm the violent pounding of my heart.

A huge old tree grew near the road, and threw an oasis of shade about itself. I went to it, sinking gratefully into the long, lush grass about its base, and I leaned against the gnarled trunk.

Gradually, I grew calmer. I had allowed a chance encounter to send me into a tailspin, goaded by the fear and anxiety of the recent past.

I took a deep breath. I was calmer now and could stand and begin the walk down the lane to the cottage at the end of it.

Mrs. Denver was mildly surprised to see me. 'Why, Karen, how nice of you to come over. Come in, please.' I followed her inside.

'I was just making some bread,' she said, leading the way into the kitchen. 'Would you like some coffee?'

I had summoned up again my sense of determination and I did not want to dissipate it on coffee and idle conversation. 'Thank you,' I said, 'but no, I didn't come here for small talk, I'm afraid.'

She eyed me warily, sizing me up, trying to gauge my mood. 'Oh?' she said, lifting an eyebrow. 'What did you come here for, then?'

'I want to talk about Emily,' I said.

It was as if I had struck her. She put a hand to her throat and stepped backward, away from me. Her other hand went to a counter top, to steady herself.

She tried, much too late, to recover. 'Emily who?' she asked in a faltering voice.

'Emily, your daughter-in-law,' I said.

'The other Mrs. Denver. Alan's first wife.'

She had managed to regain a little of her customary self-control. Her chin jutted out stubbornly. 'I have no idea who you mean,' she said.

I opened the carryall I was carrying. 'The girl who wore this gown,' I said, and threw the lace gown upon the table between us.

A little cry, like that of a trapped animal, escaped her lips, and such a look of pain distorted her face that I felt a pang of guilt at having been so brutal. But I held my ground and waited for her next ploy.

She seemed to be moving against her will, as if compelled. She went slowly to the table and a trembling hand reached out to touch the gossamer fabric lying there. She picked the gown up, letting it fall free, and her eyes studied it from top to bottom, lingering at each stain and tear. I knew she was seeing far more than I saw. I waited in determined silence for her to share her vision with me.

'So you got into that room after all,' she said finally, not even looking up at me.

'Yes,' I said.

'Despite my warnings.'

'I had to,' I cried, angry at being put on the defensive in this manner. 'I had to know.'

She did look at me then, her eyes flashing. 'And what do you know?' she demanded.

'I know that there was someone before me, someone named Emily, who wore that gown. And something terrible happened to her. I know that you can tell me the rest of it. And you must. I have a right to know the truth. *I demand it!*'

I had not realized until I stopped that I had been shouting. The silence that poured in afterward jarred.

She looked suddenly as if she would faint. She swayed and her eyes seemed to grow sightless. I rushed forward, putting a steadying arm about her.

'Here,' I said, dragging a chair away from the table with my free hand. 'Sit down, please.'

She let me guide her into the chair. Her shoulders drooped in a gesture of defeat. She brought her head down into the crook of one arm and began to sob softly. The sound gave my heart a wrench. I had recently suffered too much unhappiness of my own to want to be the cause of unhappiness in another.

When I spoke again, it was in a gentler tone.

'It's true, isn't it?' I said, laying a hand upon one trembling shoulder. 'Alan was married before, wasn't he?'

'Yes,' she said, her voice muffled by the arm on which her head lay.

'But why didn't he tell me that?'

She threw her head back so violently that my hand was knocked off her shoulder. 'Because, dear God, he doesn't remember,' she said. 'Not at all. He's blocked the entire business from his memory, and for that I give thanks every day.'

She was sobbing loudly now, tears running down her cheeks. It was a shock to see this woman, ordinarily so self-possessed, now so out of control. Her sobs verged on hysteria.

'But why?' I asked, bewildered. 'What happened? You must tell me everything.'

Her sobs became a wail. She threw her hands up as if she thought I meant to strike her. 'No, no, I can't,' she cried. 'There are things too terrible to tell, I beg you, spare me, if you've any heart at all. If it was so awful for him, think what it must have been for me, his mother. And unlike Alan, I have not forgotten, I must live with the memory, every day, for the rest of my life.'

She suddenly turned toward me and seized my hand in a grip so fierce it made me wince. Her eyes were wide and wild. 'Think what it means to a mother, to know the worst about her own son. The worst! Think how it tears my heart to tell you that you aren't safe there, in that house, with him. That's why I was so upset when he brought you here, when I learned that he had married again.'

Something crawled over the skin at the back of my neck. 'What do you mean?' I asked in as calm a voice as I could manage. 'Why am I not safe there, with him?'

She scarcely seemed to hear me. Her hysteria was growing worse with each second. She had given vent to the passions that had so long been bottled up within her, and now they raged out of control, like the waters of a mighty flood that could no longer be held back, but overran everything before them.

'You must leave there,' she sobbed, her shoulders heaving violently. 'You must, before it's too late.'

I took hold of her and shook her, trying to bring her back to reality. Something of her emotional storm had imparted itself to me, so that I felt as if I too were barely my own mistress.

'Why, in the name of God?' I demanded, shaking her cruelly. 'You must tell me, you must. What happened to Emily?'

Her sobs became a shrieking laughter that chilled the very marrow in my bones.

'He killed her,' she cried. 'Alan killed her!'

I could get nothing more from her than that. She fell forward into my arms like a rag doll, sobbing and choking. Nothing more that she said was coherent, and it was only after a long time that I was able to calm her a little.

'Let me take you to bed,' I said at last, when her sobs had become muffled whimpers. I helped her from the chair and guided her to the bedroom. She was completely passive to my commands, moving as if in a daze.

I got her into bed, and in the bathroom cabinet I found some tranquilizing pills that had been prescribed for her in the past. I made a note of the doctor's name, almost instinctively. Doctor Kramer, in Lompoc. Later I thought that I might have need of him.

For now I could only sit by the bed and pat the hand that lay limply over the covers. It was a long time before her breathing became regular and deep, and she drifted into sleep.

It was growing late. The afternoon had fled. I waited until Mrs. Denver was sound asleep. Then I let myself out of the cottage and began the long walk home. I felt certain she would be all right when she woke, and once more in possession of herself. I took the gown with me in my carryall again, not wanting to provoke another bout of that hysteria I had just witnessed.

I felt as if I too were in a daze. I had reacted to Mrs. Denver's fit of crying with instinct, remaining calm because I had to be, distracting my mind from my own fears by tending to hers.

Now, walking, with nothing to occupy my mind, I could not keep myself from considering what had just happened.

Certainly all that I had suspected had been proven true. Alan had been married, his wife's name had been Emily. Beyond any doubt, it was she who had worn the gown of rose point lace that had brought about Mrs. Denver's hysteria.

I had learned more than I bargained for, and yet not enough.

'Alan killed her!' Those awful words kept ringing in my mind.

'You aren't safe there, in that house, with him.'

It was too terrible to contemplate. Yet, there it was. I could not believe it. At the same time, how could I disbelieve it? Emily was gone. She had lost her life in some tragic way. Alan could not even remember. He had blocked everything from his mind — the entire marriage and its conclusion. His own mother had been driven to hysteria by the memory of whatever had happened.

I could not forget Alan's own reaction to the sight of that dress, nor the nightmare that had sent him in his sleep to walk the cliffs, and speak Emily's name.

If I were to believe these things, and what his mother had just told me, my husband was a murderer.

There must be some other explanation. His mother had spoken when she was nearly out of her mind, hardly in a reasonable state. And even the most obvious of clues could be read in many different ways.

Alan could tell me the truth, if I could get past the wall that he had built up in his mind. To do so, however, I invited a repeat of that awful scene from the night before, with no assurance that I would learn any more from it than I already knew.

In order to learn the story from him, I

would have to drive him also to hysteria, and having done so, how could I truly believe what I learned?

It was a house of mirrors through which I stumbled blindly, unable to distinguish the real from the illusory. Somewhere in that maze walked a woman in rose point lace, real and yet not real, only a phantom. She walked the cliffs of the Point, heard the lonely call of the foghorn. She climbed the steps to the lighthouse, and watched the light disappear into the distance over the ocean. She moved through the rooms and the halls of the house there. Perhaps she whispered to me, so softly that I could not quite hear.

Perhaps she had even beckoned me from beyond the glass, with a summoning hand.

To what would she summon me? To the same fate she had suffered? Was Mrs. Denver right? Ought I to leave the Point, while I still could? Before . . .

There I came full circle, and was back to the questions I could not answer. Before what? I neither knew what lay before me, nor behind me.

I arrived home in a despondent mood. Evening was falling. Alan was at the lighthouse, but he came in soon after I had arrived.

'How was the visit?' he asked. 'Successful?'

'A little,' I said, which was not entirely untrue. I could not tell him about it any further without launching an explanation that I did not feel up to at the moment.

He came to put his arms about me. Despite myself, I found myself cringing at his touch. My reaction filled me with dismay. This was my husband, the man I loved, not some horrible monster. I turned and kissed him fervently.

'Hey, you are in a mood,' he said when the kiss had ended. He said it in a joking manner, but I saw that his look was one of concern. I wanted to tell him then, all of my fears and doubts and questions. I very nearly did so.

I could not, of course, and I had to be brutal with myself. The thought crossed my mind that, if he went berserk again, perhaps I would not be safe.

'Sorry,' I said, and turned back to my cooking.

★   ★   ★

I slept badly that night. Each move of Alan's brought me from my fitful sleep, for all the world as if he might be trying to strangle me while I slept. Each time I discovered him sleeping quietly by my side, I felt all the more guilty for the fearful thoughts I was entertaining.

I woke in the morning feeling tired and cross, and could not seem to get my mind on any of the chores I attempted. Finally, I decided to write checks for the bills that had accumulated, and I went to the desk for them.

The desk was a big old affair that somehow gave that corner of the room a businesslike look, notwithstanding the fact that we almost never used it. I had taken to putting the household accounts in one drawer. Otherwise I rather left the piece alone.

The other drawers were filled with Alan's things, ranging from a half-finished model car in a box, to his personal papers and records. I had never had any desire to go through these — before.

I had not had any burning curiosity regarding my husband, taking it for granted that I would, as time went along learn all that I needed to know about him. I no longer had that confidence, and when I saw a sheaf of his personal papers, I knew at once what I meant to do.

I took out a stack of papers, and flipped through them. At a glance I saw nothing of great interest. There were some old letters, and I had a thought that one of them might be from a woman named Emily, but I was reluctant to read anyone's personal letters without permission.

I put them aside and looked elsewhere. I found a passport and a birth certificate, and a high school diploma, and a class photograph in which, after some indecision, I was able to pick out my husband as a teenager.

In the bottom drawer, I found a metal strongbox. It was locked, and another quick look through the drawers of the desk failed to produce a key.

I put the box on the desktop and stared at it for a long moment. It was quite an ordinary looking strongbox, the sort people often use to store their insurance papers and other documents, such as marriage certificates.

It was no good telling myself I was meddling in someone else's private business. That someone else was Alan, my husband. I wanted to help him, and myself, and our marriage. And in order to do that, I had to come to understand the past, his past. I felt certain this box might contain a clue to that past.

I took the strongbox to the kitchen with me. From here I could pry it open with a screwdriver and at the same time watch the path lest Alan come back unexpectedly.

It was not difficult to open. Inside were only a few papers of the general sort I had expected, except that none of them pertained to any marriage, or to any one named Emily.

I was about to put the box back in the desk where I had found it when I saw the corner of a photograph sticking out from between some insurance contracts. I removed the picture, turning it face up, and found myself looking at the young woman who had come to occupy my thoughts and fears so very much.

It was a picture of Emily.

7

I hadn't the slightest doubt of the identity of the woman in the picture. It was a wedding picture, and she was wearing the gown of rose point lace, with its lovely veil. The groom was not in the photograph. It was a shot taken to show off the bride and her gown, and they were both lovely. Anyway I knew all too well who the groom had been.

Even had she not been wearing the gown, however, I think I would have known that the woman in the photograph was Emily. We looked quite a bit alike in the first place. Not that I was as lovely as she, but the general resemblance was there, and fairly strong, in the shape of the face, the set of the mouth, even in the way she tilted her head to one side a little, as I was inclined to do myself. Certainly I could understand why the older man in the pickup truck, perhaps a little senile and certainly with ailing vision, could have confused me with her.

Her hair was blonde, as mine was also. It appeared from the photograph that hers was a lighter, more silvery shade than mine, and while I wore mine loose about my shoulders, she wore hers pulled back somewhat severely from her face. At least she had worn it in that style for her wedding.

It was an odd feeling to look into those eyes from the past, to see the faint smile on her lips. It was as if she had looked not into the camera, but into the future, and smiled at what she knew it would hold for me, and her smile was faintly ironic.

I felt as if I were meeting a ghost. Truly, she had haunted me since I had come to the Point. Now I was looking upon her face. I had an uneasy impression that I could turn, look over my shoulder, and see her standing behind me, smiling in that same peculiar way.

It was so strong an impression that I did indeed look over my shoulder, but the room was empty — at least so far as the eye could see.

I put the photograph away in the box,

and returned the box to the desk. There was nothing more to be uncovered, and anyway I had seen what I was looking for. At least I was no longer dealing with an invisible force, but with a threat to which I could put a face.

And Emily was a threat, in every sense of the word. She threatened me because in some way I did not yet understand, she threatened Alan. Somehow I must find a way to free him from the hold that she had over him, whatever that was.

He belonged to her still, to the past. It was she who haunted his sleep, who drove him literally out of his mind. If he was to be saved from that nightmare, it was I who must save him, and I had only one weapon with which to do it — my love for him.

I must trust in that, cling to it, take refuge in that love. If, on the other hand, I allowed it to waver, to weaken and crumble from within, Alan was doomed, and our love was doomed with him.

I was frankly afraid of another confrontation with Mrs. Denver. I knew that she could explain much to me that would help, if she chose to do so, but whatever I might learn from her would have to come voluntarily. To try to force her to my side would only create another hysterical outburst, perhaps an even worse one than yesterday's.

Yet I could not ignore her either; I had an obligation to ensure that she was all right today and in possession of herself again. There were no telephones in my house or hers, so it was necessary to pay her another visit. I took the car on this occasion, to save time. Alan was pleased to think that his mother and I were getting along so well that I paid her visits daily. I did not spoil that illusion for him.

'Well, I don't want to wear out my welcome,' I said, noncommittally. I hardly thought she would be so glad to see me again, however.

When I arrived Mrs. Denver opened the door with a sullen expression, regarding me with eyes cold as ice.

'May I come in?' I asked, since she had made no move to let me into the house.

Somewhat reluctantly, she stepped aside to let me come through the door, but she did not close the door. It seemed she was not expecting me to stay long. She needn't have worried on that score, however, as I had planned all along to make my visit a brief one.

'I hope you haven't come for a repeat of yesterday's dreadful scene,' she said.

'On the contrary, I've come to apologize for causing you such grief.'

She looked a little taken aback by that. I think she expected some ruse by which I might try to pry more information out of her.

'Very well,' she said eventually. 'I hope you understand that there are simply certain things I vowed not to tell anyone again. I think it best to let the dead bury the dead.'

'If they stay buried.' Then, seeing the anger flick into her eyes again, I added quickly, 'Oh, you needn't worry, I don't intend to bring that argument up again. I think you should tell me what you know, not for my sake alone, but for Alan's, and even for your own. But I shall respect your obviously strong feeling in the matter. I only came to apologize for yesterday, and to assure myself that you are feeling better today.'

'I am, thank you,' she said, but with little pretense at warmth or friendliness. I doubted we would ever become the friends I had once hoped we might be. In the aftermath of yesterday's stormy confrontation, I had suddenly faced something I had refused to consider before. It was not only a question of motherly resentment or jealousy. For whatever private motives, she strongly disliked me. Perhaps she even hated me.

That was only the half of it, though. She was to me like the cliffs of the Point — handsome, but in a cold, forbidding way. And like the cliffs, she was dangerous too. I thought she would let little stand in her way or prevent her from doing anything she had set her mind to do.

Of course, we both seemed to agree tacitly that, no matter how cool relations might actually be between us, it would be necessary to keep up a more or less cordial front for Alan's benefit.

'Well, goodbye then,' I said, getting ready to take my leave.

Only when I was outside the door and the visit was plainly at an end did she relent and show any faint trace of warmth.

'It was kind of you to come,' she said.

I gave her a brief smile. 'I know it may be hard for you to believe, but I never wanted to hurt you or make you unhappy. I only want to help Alan.'

'Then leave the Point,' she said abruptly, in a pleading voice. 'You simply can't do any good here and you've already caused great harm and unhappiness.'

'I won't go. Unless I can take Alan with me.'

'He'll never leave the Point. He's married to those cliffs, for as long as he lives.' *And to you*, I thought, *that's what you'd like to think*.

'Perhaps,' I said instead, 'but I am his wife and my place is with him. So long as he remains here, I shall remain here with him.'

'Do you really believe that?'

I suddenly thought that this woman, whom I had always thought so cool and self-possessed, might in fact be danger-ously unbalanced.

I found myself thinking of her belief in the ghosts said to haunt the point, of her hysteria of the day before, of her jealous possessiveness toward her son. These were not the signs of a strong, healthy mind.

'I must go.' I started up the path, back to the car.

'Don't say I didn't try to warn you,' she called after me. 'You're in grave danger there, in that house.'

Although I walked on without replying to that parting remark, it lingered in my mind on the drive home.

I had to fight constantly against the feeling that I might not be safe alone in the house with Alan. I dared not let myself believe for a moment that Alan represented any sort of physical threat to my well-being. I knew that once I gave in to that idea, our love and our marriage were doomed.

I had to find a way to free Alan. Some-how I had to make him face the past, stare it down, if he was ever to be free of it.

I thought I had an idea that might help

me. When I had gotten a tranquilizer for her from her bathroom, I had made note of the name of Mrs. Denver's doctor — Doctor Kramer, in Lompoc.

At home, I made a careful search of the medicines in our own bathroom cabinet. There wasn't much, but I found a nearly empty prescription bottle in one corner. The label told me that it contained a mild tranquilizer — butisol — and that the prescription had been written by the same Doctor Kramer in Lompoc.

I had suspected that whatever had happened here in the past, a doctor must surely have been called in. Most likely a family doctor, someone who already knew them.

I did not tell Alan where I was going. If he knew that I planned on visiting Doctor Kramer, I feared that other part of his mind might guess the reason and try to put obstacles in my path.

'Another trip into town?' he said when I mentioned the following day that I would be gone for the afternoon. 'The isolation here isn't starting to get to you, is it?'

'Not in the least. But I just haven't gotten used to the idea of taking care of everything on one trip. I keep forgetting things.' I stood on tiptoe to kiss him.

I felt guilty about deceiving him, but I reminded myself of the importance of my objective.

It was not difficult finding Doctor Kramer's office — Lompoc was rather a small town. It took only two inquiries, one at a service station coming into town and another from a woman on the street, to take me to the small house where the doctor both lived and conducted his medical practice.

A sign at the wrought iron gate directed me to a walk that led around the house, and to a side entrance. The front entrance, presumably, was for social visitors.

I came into a small, neat reception room. A bell jingled in some inner part of the house as the door opened and closed, and a moment later a tiny woman in a nurse's uniform, but with a kitchen apron over it, popped into the room. Her eyes, little and round and bright, regarded me in a cautious but not unfriendly way.

'Can I help you?' she asked.

'I'd like to see Doctor Kramer, if I may,' I said.

'Do you have an appointment?'

The question seemed a little moot, since there were no other patients in the reception room. I admitted that I had not, and I was sorry for the lack.

She was mildly disapproving. 'May I have your name and the nature of the illness?' she asked.

'I wanted to talk to the doctor about a personal matter,' I said. 'I'm Mrs. Denver.'

The little eyes grew larger. 'I see,' she said.

I had thought my evasive answer regarding the nature of my visit might provoke some discussion, but she seemed to understand that my call was indeed a personal one. Certainly she knew who I was. I wondered what she might have heard about me by way of Mrs. Scruggs and company.

'I'll see if the doctor can see you,' she said, and fairly flew out of the room.

I did not have long to wait.

A portly little man appeared in the

doorway through which the nurse, who I thought was quite probably his wife as well, had disappeared a moment before. His nose was a bulb, and his face a circle, punctuated with little round glasses that tended to slip downward. His figure had no angles, only curves.

'May I help you?' he asked, pursing his lips after speaking, so that they too formed a circle.

'Dr. Kramer?' He nodded. 'I am Mrs. Denver. Alan Denver's wife, that is.' He nodded again. 'I'd like to talk to you, if I may,' I said, since he had given me no invitation to enter the inner office that I could see behind him.

'Of course, come in, do.' He stepped gallantly aside for me, and indicated the way with a flourish of his hand.

When I had taken a seat in a plain wooden chair and he had seated himself behind his big desk, he said, 'Now then, what can I do for you?'

'I really came,' I said, choosing my words carefully, 'to talk to you about my husband.'

He nodded, but made no reply. I

decided to take the bull by the horns.

'Doctor Kramer,' I said, leaning forward in my chair, 'I believe that something has happened to my husband's memory. I think — no, I am certain — that something very unpleasant happened in the past, something that he has blocked from his mind, but that has left unpleasant after-effects. I had hoped that you might be able to tell me what did take place.'

He clapped his hands together before him and rested his elbows on the surface of his desk. 'Mrs. Denver,' he said, and I knew from the tone of voice that I had not gotten through to him. 'You surely must know that as a doctor, I have certain professional obligations to my patients. I cannot discuss a patient's case, even your husband's case, without his permission. It would simply be unethical.'

'But if he can't remember, how can he give his permission?' I sensed that he really wanted to tell me what I wanted to know. I had a feeling that there was a bit of Mrs. Scruggs in him, for all that he had his profession obligations.

'I don't believe in his present state that he even knows he came to you with any problem,' I went on. 'He's blocked things from his mind that completely. And I didn't even know myself until recently that there was a problem. To be quite frank, I didn't know until I discovered it by chance that he had even been married before he married me.'

'I rather thought you wouldn't know that,' he said, smiling faintly as if to encourage me.

'Then you do know that his memory is gone, at least regarding this incident.'

'Naturally.' He leaned back in his chair, patting his round tummy, and looked at me over the rim of his spectacles. 'You mentioned some after-effects. What sort of after-effects did you mean?'

'For one thing, and I think you will agree it's a very serious thing, he nearly killed himself on the cliffs at the Point.' I saw that this had hit home, and I pursued my advantage. 'I found a gown that had been worn by his first wife, by Emily. When I showed it to him, Alan went berserk. He ran from the house, toward the cliffs. I believe he would have thrown himself over them if I hadn't screamed, and he fainted. And when he recovered, he had no memory of that incident either.'

'That certainly is serious,' he said thoughtfully.

'And that isn't all. He's having nightmares, and walking in his sleep. Another night I found him sleepwalking on the cliffs. One false step and he might have died on that occasion. Doctor Kramer, Alan might not remember what happened in the past, but it's there, in his mind, and it is haunting him. I truly believe it will lead to further tragedy unless I can do something to help him, and I can't help him unless I know the truth of what happened. Don't you see that?'

'What does his mother say of all this?'

I sighed. 'She's as frightened of whatever happened in the past as he is. She refused to talk to me of it. When I tried to make her tell me, she became hysterical and warned me that Alan might be dangerous.'

'Dangerous in what way?' he asked, watching me intently.

'She said that he had killed Emily, and that he might try to kill me too,' I said, forcing myself to meet his questioning gaze.

He nodded and looked down at his clasped hands. In the pause that followed, I could hear the loud ticking of a clock on the wall behind me, seeming to issue its own warning. Beyond the window, a bird sang, sounding unconcerned.

'Yet knowing this,' he said finally, 'you've remained there?'

'I love my husband. I have no fear of him, only fear for him.'

He smiled. I think something about my attitude pleased him. He got up and went to the window, closing it and shutting out the song of the bird, and, perhaps, any eavesdropper who might happen to hear what he was about to say.

'The truth is, my dear girl, almost anyone in town could tell you what you want to know, at least part of it. People spoke of nothing else for weeks. So I suppose there's really no professional violation in my telling you, and I can prevent your getting some garbled version of the story.'

'Then you'll tell me what happened?'

'Yes, I will,' he said, and sat himself at the desk again.

* * *

The story that Doctor Kramer told me was a long one; one of intense drama. He spoke of love, sacred and illicit, of hate and fear and madness, of violence and finally of death. All of it made more dramatic, more tragic, by the mundane way in which he related them.

'I did treat Alan for injuries in an accident, better than a year ago,' he said. 'I got a call one night from his mother. Frankly, she was in a fit. I could hardly tell what had happened from the way she was carrying on. She had driven down the road to the nearest house with a phone. I always thought there should be a phone at the Point. It's just too isolated up there to be without one, but neither she nor

Alan had ever heeded my advice on that score.

'I went right there, of course, even though it was past my office hours. A good doctor has to go when he's needed, whether it is personally convenient or not.'

He paused, and thinking that I was expected to comment on this, I murmured, 'It's good of you to take that attitude.'

He beamed at me, cleared his throat, and went on. 'She wasn't much calmer when I got there. I thought it was she I was coming to treat, but it wasn't, it was Alan. He'd fallen on the cliff, banged himself up pretty badly, with one especially bad cut on the head. Here, on the temple.' He indicated the place.

'Yes,' I said, 'he still has a scar there — but he couldn't remember how he had gotten it. He seemed, in fact, not to know it was there until I mentioned it.'

'That is peculiar, that he would be unaware of it,' he said. 'But I'm getting ahead of myself, though. I ought to start at the beginning, which was his marriage.

When they got married, it was big news here in town, of course. It's a good ways from here, but the people in town look upon the Point as part of the town, and anything that goes on up there interests the women locally, you understand.'

Like Mrs. Scruggs, I thought, but did not say.

'Anyway, everyone was fond of Alan, he's a likeable young man, and they were happy to see him wed. And they seemed to like Emily well enough, too, at least in the beginning. She was a pretty girl, I'll say that. Looked a bit like you, as a matter of fact. But not a lot, either.' He studied me critically for a moment. 'You look like you've got courage. Emily was like a little wildflower that you knew would never survive being replanted. Pretty, but fragile, if you get what I mean.'

'And replanting to the Point — that could be a challenge to someone without a lot of backbone. It is so isolated.'

'Exactly. Anyway, from what my wife heard, they had met and gotten married awful quick-like. That wasn't hard to understand, of course. As you say, the

Point is so isolated. It must get very lonely for a man up there. Alan's mother kept a close eye on him, but even so a man wants more than that. And, to make a long story short, he was on leave, he met Emily, and the first thing you know, she's back here as his bride.'

I felt a pang. It was so like what had happened with Alan and me. History repeating itself — or, rather, Alan repeating himself, but apparently without knowing he was doing so.

As if reading my thoughts, he said, 'It was much the same with you, wasn't it?'

'Yes,' I said tersely, nodding.

He went on, 'I think that part of it, the quickness, was Alan was trying to assert his independence. His mother tends to be a bit possessive, as I am sure you have taken note, and he doesn't seem to be the sort of man to tolerate that indefinitely.

'But what Alan didn't know, unfortunately, was that Emily wasn't quite right.' He tapped the side of his head with a finger. 'Oh, she wasn't crazy, not really, but she had a long history of instability, as I learned later. She'd been in a hospital three different times with difficulties. What the layman would term nervous breakdowns. I learned about them when she began coming to see me.'

'Then she was your patient, too.'

'Yes. And again, I am violating no confidence. This too is common knowledge around town. She had all sorts of complaints, mysterious aches and pains, which she would share with anyone who would listen, and some who tried not to. One time she was limping so badly it seemed she could hardly walk, although she managed to get all over town. There was simply nothing to it, except in her head. The loneliness up there, and the isolation, you see.'

'I can see how it could wear on someone already a bit nervous.'

'Exactly. It's all right for a healthy person, I expect you handle it perfectly well, but it began to prey on her. She started with a multitude of nonexistent ailments. I did what I could for her, but when I started to look into her history, I knew it was a mistake for her to be there, a big mistake.'

'That poor thing,' I said.

He nodded. 'Yes. I talked to her, of course. I even talked to Alan, but you see, he had lived there all his life, grown up with it. He saw nothing hard about it. And, he himself was not much more than a kid, a healthy one at that. It was just too difficult for him to understand what it was doing to his wife. Perhaps if I had been more forceful, more dramatic, in describing her history . . . but I didn't want to betray her confidence, you understand, everything she had told me about her history, about the nervous breakdowns, was told in confidence, was meant to be private between the two of us. I could only hint at it, and he never quite caught on. I suppose that sort of thing was just so far outside his own experience.'

I wondered. It seemed to me as if Alan was having some sort of breakdown of his own — but of course, what the doctor was describing had all transpired earlier.

'Anyway, he remained convinced that she would adjust to the situation in time, if she would just stop imagining things so much. And that was another problem. Somehow she had heard about ghosts that are supposed to haunt the cliffs. It was all a lot of nonsense, any sane person would scoff at it. But she wasn't quite sane. At least, she started taking the stories seriously, she began to think she was seeing and hearing things.'

'What sort of things?' I asked uneasily.

He waved a hand in the air as if the very idea irritated him profoundly. 'Voices calling her outside at night, people tapping at the window . . . is it cold in here?'

I had shivered involuntarily. I pulled my shoulders back and said, 'No, that's all right. Go on, please.'

'Well,' he said, leaning back in his chair again, 'that sort of talk only aggravated Alan. He laughed at her, said she was crazy. Which was the wrong thing to say to her, but he didn't know. Mind you, I don't think he meant to be cruel. He just didn't understand how her mind worked. When she tried to talk him into going away, giving up the job, he got sore and told her he had heard all he wanted to hear about ghosts and loneliness and moving away, and that was that.'

I could quite imagine Alan taking that approach. He had not accepted that someone or something had locked me into the lighthouse. He had little truck with ghosts.

'Of course, that wasn't the end of it, not by any means. There was another man up at the point then, another lighthouse keeper. Not Farroday, he didn't come until later. This man's name was Walt something or other. Benton, I think. A big, good-looking man, sort of rugged, you know.

'I suppose what happened next was inevitable, she being so lonesome, needing someone to talk to. I imagine by then she was scared of her own shadow. She told me she couldn't sleep at all when Alan was out of the house, when he had to work nights at the lighthouse. She would lie awake all night until he came in and then try to nap during the day. I really think that, toward the end, she was scared out of her wits most of the time. The last time I saw her, she looked like she hadn't slept in a week.

'I don't know exactly what happened. It seemed as if she started crying on Walt's shoulder. She was one to need to cry on someone's shoulder, and I don't think she found Alan's welcoming any longer. But I'm only surmising that.

'What did happen was that Alan's mother called me that night to come up there. She was hysterical and Alan was out cold with a mean gash in his head.'

'And Emily?'

'Emily was dead. She was on the rocks, at the bottom of the cliff.'

I gasped, even though I had half suspected this was how the story would end. In my mind I saw the cliffs, with their jagged rocks, the waves pounding below. I remembered a moment when I had felt myself slipping, had thought that I would surely fall to my death.

'When I finally got his mother settled down a bit, she told me that Alan had come to her house early that evening in a rage. He had learned that things were going on between his wife and Walt. There had been a violent scene between his wife and him, during which — mind you, I'm repeating this third hand — during which he struck her.

'While he was telling his mother about it — and again, I can only repeat what she told me — he was drinking heavily. Finally, still in a rage and drunk to boot, he staggered out of her house to go home and have it out with Walt.

'It was an awful night, storming like the dickens. I expect you've been there long enough to know how a storm can blow up there. The rain was coming down in sheets and the wind was near hurricane force. Nobody but a madman or a doctor would go out on a night like that.

'She went after him. When she got there, Emily and Alan were on the cliff. Emily had put on her wedding gown. The strain had apparently been too much for her. She was trying to throw herself over the cliff and Alan was trying to hold her back. She got loose from him and ran for the edge. He went after her but he stumbled and fell. It was wet and dark and he was still feeling all that liquor. She went over and he hit his head on the rocks, and never got up.'

'How awful,' I said. A sense of horror had come over me. I felt as if I had lived through the tragic night.

'Walt was gone, cleared out. No one ever saw or heard of him again. From the looks of his place, he and Alan had had quite a row.

'No one ever got any details out of Alan, because when he did come to, he didn't remember a thing about any of it. He didn't even remember Emily. The name meant nothing to him. I thought maybe it was the crack on his head — it had been a pretty nasty one.'

'Did no one investigate further?'

'Of course, the sheriff did. There was some talk that maybe Alan was faking his amnesia, so I persuaded him to see a psychiatrist friend of mine down in Santa Barbara. He said Alan was carrying a big load of guilt over having ignored Emily's pleas, and feeling as if he had driven her to her death. He had just plain closed a door in his mind on the whole thing, and he has never opened it again as far as I know.'

I hated asking the question that I asked next, but it had to be asked. 'Was there any suspicion that Alan might have . . . ?' I could not bring myself to finish it.

'Might have murdered her?' Doctor Kramer finished for me. I nodded. He shook his head. 'He fell a good ways back from the edge, and that was where he was still lying when I got there, unless somebody had moved him. It's possible, but I don't think so.'

His story was at an end. We sat in silence for a moment.

'Is there no way to open those doors in Alan's mind?' I asked eventually. 'To force him to remember?'

He took a long deep breath and exhaled it slowly. 'I'm no psychiatrist,' he said. 'Although I think I know pretty well how men's minds work. I suspect that some great shock would probably jar him enough to bring it all back. Apparently once or twice you've come close to doing that already, but don't you see, there's no telling what may happen as a result. You said he seemed about to kill himself on one occasion. He might actually do that, driven by his guilt. Or he might try to . . . ' He paused, on the verge of saying something that he decided not to say. 'There's just no telling what he might try to do.'

'Still, I think I have to try.'

'You seem to have overlooked something,' he said, looking me straight in the eye. 'Don't you see the similarities between your situation and Emily's? The sudden marriage, your physical resemblance to Emily. It could be nothing more than mere coincidence, but it could be too that Alan is trying to relive the entire tragic episode, with you playing the role of Emily. And if that is so, there's no guessing how it will end this time.'

'But Alan didn't really harm Emily,' I said.

'He believes he did. He thinks that he killed her. Don't you see where this could be leading you?'

8

I thanked the good doctor for his time and left. 'You're a very brave woman,' he said as we were parting.

I did not feel at all brave, though. I felt shaken by the story I had heard. I felt as if I had played a part in that tragic chain of events. The ghost of Emily still haunted me, but she was no longer threatening. She was a pathetic apparition. I mourned for her loneliness and her sadness. How the isolation of the point, with its storms and winds and pounding waves, must have weighed upon her, wearing her down as the elements eroded the rocks and the cliffs. It had become a nightmare for her, a nightmare from which she had never awakened.

And Alan — I could understand his role in the story as well. His had not been a heartless, deliberate cruelty, but the cruelty of uncomprehending youth. If he had been truly heartless he would have suffered not at all from guilt afterward. If only I could somehow free him from that guilt. Until I did so, Emily would continue to torture him with her memory.

How could I free him, though, faced with the fear that my very efforts to do so might bring about his destruction? I was not afraid for myself, despite what Doctor Kramer had said. Alan had not truly murdered his wife and somewhere within himself he knew that, if only I could make him face it. If he once faced the truth, I was confident everything else would fall into its proper perspective.

At least, this was what I believed most of the time, but despite my best efforts, I suffered doubts as well, moments when I wondered.

Alan's mother obviously believed that he had killed Emily. This was clearly different from what she had told Doctor Kramer. She had not spoken to me of an accident in which Emily had fallen, or had thrown herself over the cliff.

She had told me flat out that Alan had killed his wife, and she had warned me that it might not be safe for me to remain with Alan. She had told me she knew 'the worst' about her son, and that knowledge had driven her to hysteria.

These thoughts buzzed through my mind like so many troublesome insects, around and around.

Because I had needed an excuse to make the trip to town, I had armed myself with a short list of purchases to make. On the list was a new pen to replace the one that had stopped writing for me a few days before.

For this I made a stop at the same stationery store I had gone to before. The same woman waited on me, but whereas before she had been friendly and outgoing, this time her manner toward me was quite changed. She looked, in fact, somewhat startled to see me come into her shop again.

'Hello,' I greeted her, making an effort to sound cheerful despite the grim story Doctor Kramer had just shared with me. 'Remember me?'

'Yes, of course,' she said. She did not return my smile and she avoided looking at me directly.

A bit puzzled, I told her what I wanted and she rather rudely clapped three pens down upon the counter for my inspection. I had an impression she thought I was carrying some disease, which she might get from too close contact with me. The change in her behavior mystified and depressed me.

I selected a pen, giving it no real thought, and paid her. She gave me my change without thanking me. I came close to asking if I had done something to merit her disapproval. In fact, I had opened my mouth to say something, but she seemed to realize I was on the verge of frankness.

'Excuse me,' she said and hurried off to a back room, leaving me alone in the shop.

It was only another of the puzzlements confronting me, but not the most important of them. I left the shop feeling disheartened, but the coolness of the saleswoman was quickly replaced in my mind by the memory of my conversation with Doctor Kramer. It was that conversation that occupied my thoughts on the drive back to the Point, so that by the time I had arrived home, I had all but forgotten the visit to the stationery store.

Something occurred soon after that visit into town that brought vividly back to mind Doctor Kramer's parting remarks.

I had baked a cake for Alan and, meaning to be friendly and to repay Farroday for his help when I had needed him, I took a large slice of the cake to his cottage.

I had no reservations about going to Farroday's quarters. I did not in any way look upon him as a threat or a danger. On the contrary, he had proven to be a friend when I needed him and I thought that should I really be in a spot, I could call on him and count on his help.

He was pleased with the gift and thanked me warmly. 'It's nothing, really,' I assured him. 'I wanted to thank you for helping me that night with Alan, and for not saying anything about it to him.'

'You're still worrying about what went on here before you came?' he asked.

'Yes. I know quite a bit more about it, but I still don't know what to do now.'

'Maybe you ought to do nothing.

Sometimes that's the best policy.'

'Sometimes,' I agreed. 'But I think the time is past in this situation where that might work. I think trouble is on the horizon, unless I can find a way to fend it off.'

I sighed and smiled. 'But that's not your problem. I hope you enjoy the cake.'

'Well, thanks again,' he said, seeing me to the door. 'And if you need a hand in the future, you let me know, okay?'

'Thanks,' I said, and left. That was the extent of our conversation and of my visit.

Later, however, Alan commented upon it. 'Did I see you going down to Farroday's cottage this morning?' he asked. I thought it was only an idle question, and I replied without concern.

'Umm hum. I thought he might like a piece of that cake I baked yesterday.'

'You haven't forgotten he's a bachelor, have you?' he asked. 'Think what the neighbors might say, a married woman like yourself calling upon a single man like Farroday, in his house, no less.'

'But, darling,' I said, 'there are no neighbors to notice.'

Alan had made his remarks in a teasing fashion, but something in his voice gave me pause. Was I only imagining it, or was there an undercurrent of tension, a warning note?

At first I thought surely I must be mistaken. I had never given Alan any reason to be jealous of me, and certainly it was ridiculous to think he might be jealous of me and Farroday. It would take a madman to think he saw any sign of intimacy between us.

Or, I reminded myself later, when the conversation had been brought to a joking conclusion, a man obsessed with something that had happened in the past. I remembered later what had happened with Alan's first wife and the man who had been his co-worker at that time.

I remembered as well what Doctor Kramer had said before I left him: 'It could be that Alan is trying to relive the entire tragic episode . . . '

Had Alan only been joking? Or was he, as the doctor had suggested, recreating that sorry affair between Emily and Walt, with Farroday and I cast in the roles of the ill-fated lovers?

The more I considered this possibility, the more frightening it became. Was Alan preparing himself mentally for another jealous rage, directed this time at Farroday and me, as the other had been directed at Walt and Emily?

The prospect began to haunt me. I found myself watching Alan carefully, especially when Farroday was close at hand — or even when Farroday came into the conversation. Little remarks began to take on a worrisome significance.

'It seems to me you like Farroday a bit, don't you?' Alan said on one occasion.

I tried to sound offhanded in my reply. 'I suppose so,' I said. 'He's a likable sort. Thank Heaven.'

'What do you mean by that?' Was it only my imagination or was there a hard edge to his voice?

'Just that it would be rather awkward, wouldn't it, if he and I didn't get along?' I replied. 'I mean, we are rather cast off up here. It's almost as if we were on a desert island, the three of us.'

This remark, far from satisfying him, only seemed to make him more uneasy. 'I guess the isolation and the loneliness must be getting to you. It's hard for a woman.'

'Is it?' I asked. 'I can't say I particularly noticed.'

Yet another time he worried about Farroday's lack of feminine companionship. 'It's too bad he doesn't have a wife of his own,' he said. 'It's awfully lonely up here for a single man. It must be even harder for him now that I've got a wife. He can't help being a little envious, I suppose.'

With the necessity of parrying thee questions, I was only vaguely aware that something was amiss between myself and Mrs. Scruggs. She was unaccountably cool toward me on her next visit — not unfriendly, so much as wary. It troubled me a little. I thought it might have to do with the fact that I had not shared the full story of the rose point gown with her.

It was Alan, however, with whom I was mostly concerned during this period.

I tried to make light of his hints

regarding Farroday, to remain casual and unconcerned, but increasingly I felt myself being cast in a mold that had been created in the past. I felt as if I were caught up in a swift current that swept me on toward a rocky destination, and from which I could not free myself.

* * *

For a time I seemed to be drifting helplessly. I could not think what I should do. Every course of action available to me appeared fraught with danger, and I hesitated indecisively while events about me formed themselves into shapes that grew increasingly threatening.

Doctor Kramer had remarked upon the similarities between my story and Emily's. He did not know the full truth, however. He did not know that there was yet another point of similarity between our experiences.

Emily had thought she was haunted by the ghosts said to roam the Point. The doctor scoffed and thought the things she had seen and heard to be only the product of her tortured mind.

He did not know that I had seen a hand at the window, for one thing, or about the time I found myself locked in the lighthouse, which later was clearly unlocked. And I was soon given another proof that the ghosts that haunted our cliffs were real and a danger to me.

The fears that now beset me had produced something of a paradox in my relations with Alan. On one hand, I felt as if a wedge were being driven between us, attempting to drive us apart. Yet at the same time I felt in another way as if I were closer to him. I tried to stay near him physically, to watch his every move. I thought perhaps his behavior would give me some clue as to which way I should go with our problem and I studied him carefully, watching for that clue.

I had even taken to watching him at work, as it were. Often when he was working at the lighthouse, I would stroll over, in part to assure him that I was not involved with Farroday at the time, but really just to be close at hand. I tried to stay out of the way, and I chatted inconsequentially with him while I was there. Sometimes I would come over when he was due to return to the house, and stroll back with him.

There were times when Alan and I might have been any normal young married couple — happy, in love, living an ordinary life from day to day. He seemed often to be unaffected by the dangers that threatened us. He was not consciously aware of them, whatever his subconscious mind might be brewing for us.

Sometimes even I forgot my troubles.

This was one such night. He had stayed late, replacing some wiring at the lighthouse which, like everything else here, was quickly aged and eroded by the wind and salt air. I had come over to watch him while he finished the job, and when it was done, we strolled back to the house in a leisurely fashion.

We were near the house when it happened. From out of the night came the voice of a woman, calling faintly but distinctly, 'Alan.'

It was a summons, a plea. In the

213

darkness, with the wind up and howling over the crags, it was difficult to say from where it had come. It might almost have been a part of the wind, to come from nowhere and everywhere. It was eerie, and frightening.

We both stopped in our tracks. Instinctively I grasped Alan's arm, clinging to him. I thought of the hand that I had seen at the window, summoning me — almost to my death.

It came again, long and low, rushing down upon the gale. 'Alan.'

Beside me, Alan whispered a reply — one word, but it turned my blood cold and made me tighten my grip on his arm.

'Emily,' he said.

I looked into his face and saw that he was transfixed. His eyes were wide, staring into the distance, as if they saw more than I could see, more than the rocks and the cliffs and our house in the distance with its welcoming lights yellow against the night. He looked as he had looked that night he walked in his sleep, like he was in another world.

'Alan,' I pleaded with him, 'don't listen.

It's nothing; it's only the wind playing tricks on us.'

'No, it's Emily,' he said as if in a trance.

Again that voice came, ghostly and terrifying, calling his name. It sounded fainter now, more distant. I prayed that whatever it might be was going away, and that I could somehow coax Alan inside with me, to safety.

'Alan, please,' I begged, tugging at his arm. 'Come in with me.'

It felt as if we stood on the threshold between two worlds. Before us, not so far away and yet seemingly separated from us by an abyss, was the realm of light, where the powers of evil could not touch us. Here we stood in the realm of darkness, and I could almost feel evil sweeping about us, embracing us, claiming us for its own.

I was not only clinging to Alan's physical being. I was fighting now for his soul, and I threw out my love as if it were a solid thing, a wall that could shield us from the evil forces that threatened.

The evil had already taken hold of him, and even now was prying him loose from me. Alan pulled his arm free of my grasp and stumbled in the direction from which the cry had seemed to come.

'Emily,' he called loudly, 'where are you?' He began to run into the night.

'Oh, God,' I sobbed, throwing back my head, lifting my face to Heaven, 'help me.' Then I ran after him.

It was a nightmare from which it seemed I would never waken. The house and its lights fell behind us, and there was only darkness and the howling wind and that horrible voice that came from hell itself, from beyond the grave. Always it was far away, a will-o-the-wisp that we pursued in vain.

'Alan,' it called, and he ran blindly after it, calling in reply, 'Emily, where are you?'

I could do nothing but run after him, my legs aching, my lungs feeling as if they were on fire from the effort. I stumbled on the rocks, scraping my knees and bruising an elbow, but I scrambled to my feet and ran on.

How long or how far we ran I could not guess. It was unreal, beyond the realm of sensory perception. At last my strength was exhausted. We had run along the cliffs, following their torturous path. Before us the ground rose, then fell again. I saw Alan silhouetted for a moment against the sky as he mounted the little hill. He staggered as if he were drunk and disappeared over the hill, out of my sight.

My foot slipped and I fell. I could not summon the strength to get up again. My limbs refused to obey my commands. My chest was heaving with the effort of breathing and my sides might have been on fire.

I dropped my head into the crook of my arm and began to cry. Between sobs I prayed for the strength to go on. I prayed that Alan would be all right. I prayed that the ghostly voice would be silenced.

How long I lay there I had no idea. My heart began gradually to slow its pounding that had threatened to break through my ribs. Finally I was able to breathe without gasping frantically for the air.

At length I realized that the night had fallen silent. The wind still roared and not far away I could still hear the pounding of the ocean's waves, but I heard no nightmare voice calling Alan's name — nor his frantic replies.

I did not know what that silence meant, nor what lay before me over the hill. I managed to get shakily to my feet and stumbled on.

9

I reached the top of the little hill. The ground sloped downward before me.

At first I saw nothing ahead and a new wave of fear lashed over me. It gave me the strength to hurry on.

I nearly stumbled over Alan. He had fallen to the ground in a heap. In the first seconds of discovery, I thought of every horrible possibility, but he was alive, apparently unhurt. His tortured mind must have shut itself off as it had before, or perhaps he had driven himself to the end of his strength and had merely collapsed.

He might have caught up with his ghost and met it face to face. I did not know whether I prayed this was so, or prayed that it had not happened.

In our crazed chase through the night, we had come almost to his mother's cottage, along the cliff path that I had found frightening even in daylight. I could do nothing with Alan's unconscious body myself. I left him lying there and hurried on to his mother's house.

Luckily she was up and answered my frantic knocking almost at once. 'Karen, my goodness, what are you doing here?' she asked and then, seeing my frenzied state, she said anxiously, 'What's wrong? Something's happened.'

'Alan,' I managed to croak, still all out of breath. 'I left him along the path. He's unconscious.'

Whatever faults Mrs. Denver might have, she was a woman of decisive action. She did not waste time on a lot of questions. 'I'll get a light,' she said. She disappeared inside, to reappear a moment later. She had brought not only a flashlight, but a folded sheet of canvas as well.

Alan was still unconscious where I had left him. His mother quickly unfolded the canvas on the ground beside him. 'Help me roll him over onto this,' she said, 'it'll make it easier for us to carry him back to the house.'

We pushed and tugged and between

the two of us managed to roll him onto the canvas. Using that as a kind of stretcher, we were able to carry and drag him to the house. It gave me a sense of relief to have him safely inside, in the light. I had not heard that ghostly voice again, but so long as we were outside and Alan was unconscious, I felt that he was still in danger.

The two of us managed to get him, still dressed, into bed. At last, confident that he was all right, we retired to the kitchen.

'I'll reheat the coffee,' she said, getting cups down from the cupboard. 'I think you'd better tell me what happened.'

I did, the entire story, while we sipped coffee at her kitchen table. For the present the animosity that existed between us was set aside. We had a common interest in Alan's well-being that overrode all other considerations. I knew, regardless of what she thought about me, that she cared about him.

When I had finished my story, she said, 'So, now you too have come to accept our ghosts as real.'

I frowned and tried to put my own

thoughts into some sort of order. 'I don't know,' I said. 'I heard something. And before, I saw something, but what they were, I can't tell you.'

'You don't have to. I know, and I'm not afraid to admit the truth.'

A noise from the other room made us both start and turn in that direction. Alan appeared in the doorway. He looked sleepy, and more than a little bewildered.

'Hello,' he said, looking from one to the other of us. 'What am I doing here?'

'Don't you remember?' I asked him quickly.

He tried to think but no look of comprehension lighted his expression. 'Sorry,' he said with a rueful grin, 'but I can't. I remember us starting for the house, but then . . . '

'You got sick,' his mother explained for me, asserting her authority. 'Karen came for me and we brought you here where I could keep an eye on you.'

He sank into a chair beside me. I could see that he was wrestling with the mystery of his sickness. I had not observed his doing this before, and I felt a quickening of my pulse. If he were starting to question the peculiarities of his behavior, the things he could not remember, that must have left blanks in his consciousness, there might be hope after all.

The effort seemed, nevertheless, to be too great for him. He sighed and shook his head.

'I just don't remember a thing,' he said, giving his mother an apologetic look. To me he said, 'I guess we'd better be getting home.'

'You can stay here if you like,' Mrs. Denver said at once. 'Karen could bring the car over for you in the morning and . . .'

'Oh,' I interrupted this suggestion, 'I think the night air might help Alan. We'll walk back along the road.'

'I only thought . . . he has been sick, after all,' she said, a petulant note creeping into her voice.

'Well, I feel fine now,' Alan said, standing and stretching. 'I think you're right, honey, the night air will be good for me. I guess we'd better be on our way.'

Although his manner was casual, something about the tone of his voice gave me fresh hope. I had an idea that he had made note of the discord between his mother and me, her attempts to dominate him at my expense, and that he had put himself on my side.

We walked most of the way home in silence, but the mystery of his behavior seemed to linger on Alan's mind. When we were nearly there, he asked out of the blue, 'What's wrong with me?'

I was so surprised that I paused in mid-step, and had to hurry to catch up with him. 'What do you mean?' I asked.

He shrugged and said, 'I don't know. I just feel strange. I keep thinking there's something I ought to remember, like a name that you've got on the tip of your tongue, but I can't quite get it.'

I did not want to push him over the brink into full memory, however. I already knew that course was filled with dangers. Instead, I hedged. 'Whatever it is, I'm sure it will come back to you.'

We reached home without any incidents. I did not realize until we were inside the house and I had begun to relax a little, just how tense and frightened I had been during the walk home. The ghosts seemed to have decided to rest for the night, however.

I fell asleep, determined to put them to sleep once and for all. I thought I knew just how I would do it, too. I had a plan, finally. I was done with inaction. It was not a course to which I was accustomed, nor with which I was comfortable. I had always believed in taking the bull by the horns.

Mrs. Denver came to call on me in the morning. I thought at first she had come to check on Alan, and I was quick to tell her, 'Alan's working. He's feeling fine this morning. No ill effects.'

'This time,' she said drily. She came into the kitchen where I had been working and put her purse rather noisily atop the table. 'I came to talk to you, as a matter of fact.'

'Did you?' She had a determined look about her, but I did not mean to let her intimidate me. 'If you've come to tell me the story of Emily and what happened here, I may as well tell you, I've already heard it.'

It was her turn to raise an eyebrow. 'From whom?'

'I saw Doctor Kramer. He told me the entire story.'

She smiled in a mysterious way. 'So far as he knows it, you mean.' She became serious again. 'Well, then, you must see for yourself how imperative it is that you leave the Point.'

'I'm afraid I don't follow you.'

'Don't be a fool,' she snapped. 'If you won't think of your own safety, think of Alan's well-being. Look what has happened since you came here. He was fine until then, but since you arrived, there have been all sorts of unpleasant incidents. And they are getting worse.'

I had to admit that what she said was true. My presence here did indeed seem to have made things worse, if only by virtue of reviving the memories he had been able to forget.

She seemed to sense my line of thought and seized upon it eagerly to make her point. 'It wouldn't have to be forever, you see,' she said. 'Only until Alan can get things worked out in his mind, and get over that entire unfortunate incident. Then, when he's well again, and that's something we both desire, why, he could come to you, wherever you are.'

She paused, narrowing her eyes shrewdly. 'Who knows,' she said, 'perhaps by then your feelings will have changed. You're young, and beautiful. There are surely many men who would be happy to devote their lives to you. Why should you settle for the twisted past that Alan can offer you?'

'Because it's Alan I love. And my place is with him, no matter what sort of difficulties he's having.'

Her shrewdness dissolved into anger. 'And you don't care if you destroy him?'

'I think he is being destroyed,' I said, unmoved by her anger. 'And I'm determined to save him.'

'You don't understand him.'

'I understand that he's enslaved by the past. His guilt is devouring him from within. He blames himself for Emily's death, and so long as he's unable to face what really happened, his guilt will remain and grow worse. He has to be forced to face that past. And I know how

227

I'm going to do it. I mean to bring that past to life.'

'How?'

'By confronting him with the one person most involved in it. Emily.'

She snorted her disdain. 'Emily is dead and gone.'

'Dead, yes, but not gone. She's still here in spirit, haunting him, haunting us.'

'And what do you plan to do?' she asked, her lips curling in a sneer, 'hold a séance and conjure her up?'

'I won't have to do that.' I reached behind my head and grabbed my long blonde hair, twisting it back and up so that it was pulled severely back from my face. I smiled at her as Emily had smiled from the photograph in the desk.

She reeled as if I had struck her, her eyes going wide. 'You're mad. He'll kill you.'

'I don't believe that. And I'm willing to take that risk. If I fail to break the spell that she holds over him, I'll do as you ask, and go away.'

She snatched up her purse from the table and strode angrily to the door, but there she paused to turn back. Her eyes were flashing and she looked on the verge of madness in that moment. She was beside herself with a fury that seemed to me unwarranted.

'I warn you,' she said. 'What you are doing is not only foolish, it's dangerous. Take my advice, leave now, today. I'll make it all right with Alan.'

I shook my head firmly. 'I won't be frightened away,' I said.

'Very well. Then whatever happens, just remember that you brought it down upon your own head.'

With that she went out, banging the door shut after her.

* * *

The scene with Mrs. Denver had left me troubled. I had a strange feeling that she was not completely rational at the present time. I felt that she had truly pitted herself against me and that we were now engaged in a fierce struggle, with Alan as the prize.

For the present, however, I had other

enemies with which to contend. The idea of impersonating Emily had occurred to me the night before, and the more I thought of it the more right it seemed to me.

Alan needed some sort of great shock to restore his memory. He'd had shocks before, but they had resulted in his running away from his memories, or in pursuit of Emily. This time Emily, or at least the impersonation of her, would be right there before him. He could not avoid confronting her.

I felt confident that once his memory had come back to him, he could be made to understand what had happened, and his part in it, and thus could eventually overcome the guilt that troubled him. None of this could happen, though, until he faced the past squarely. I was hoping desperately that the sight of Emily, as she had appeared on that fateful night, would accomplish this.

I knew that Alan planned to work late that evening. He came home briefly for dinner and then went back to the lighthouse. This, I thought, was the ideal time to put my plan into action. A storm was coming up and even this seemed to be a favorable sign. It had stormed the night of the tragedy with Emily. The sameness of the weather would help bring the past to life for him.

When Alan had gone out again, I went to our room and began to make ready. I got the gown of rose point lace down from the closet where I had hidden it from him, and put it on. It fit as if it had been made for me, and I thought again, with a slight pang of anxiety, how similar Emily and I had been in appearance.

I had only the memory of that one photograph to go by, but from that I thought that Emily had tended toward pale make-up. I experimented with my own make-up until I had achieved much the same look.

When I had tied my hair back tightly from my face, and studied myself in the dressing table mirror, I looked strikingly like that haunted young woman from the past. Given Alan's emotional turmoil and the help of the semi-darkness, I thought the effect would be striking.

Alan had said he would be at the lighthouse for no more than an hour. When it was nearly time for him to be starting home, I let myself quietly out the back door.

I stood for a moment in the darkness outside, sheltering in the doorway. It had begun to rain earlier, and now that rain had become a downpour. I was frightened by what lay before me, and for a moment my courage threatened to fail me. A flash of lightning illuminated the view for a brief instant and gave it an unearthly look.

I found myself thinking of the real Emily. Had she been haunting the Point? What would the ghosts who were supposed to roam here think, seeing me usurp their place?

In the distance I saw the sweep of a flashlight beam. Alan was coming up the wooden steps from the lighthouse. There was no more time to consider the wisdom of what I had planned.

I stepped from the shelter of the doorway and ran out into the rain. I ran to a point near the cliff's edge, where the path led from the steps to the house, and stopped, standing motionless, the rain beating down on me. The dress was drenched already, clinging to me coldly, as it must have clung to Emily on the night of her death. The rain in my face made a blur of things.

The beam of Alan's flashlight came before him and then, as he got closer, I could see the gleam of his slicker. He was looking down, and might have gone by where I stood without ever noticing me, but when he was about to pass me, I softly spoke his name.

'Alan.'

His head jerked up and about and he saw me. The flashlight fell from his hands, clattering to the ground, and went out. In its wake, the night seemed darker than ever.

'Emily?' he said, his voice that of a small boy — bewildered, even frightened.

I held out a hand to him. 'I've been waiting for you,' I said.

He came toward me slowly, moving as if his feet were leaden. He reached out for me, grasping my shoulders, and bent me back so that my face was turned up to him. He looked down at me. I knew that illusion was battling with reality in his mind.

It seemed as if we stood there for hours, though it could only have been a few seconds. I was not so brave that I did not remember the warnings of Doctor Kramer and Alan's mother. The cliffs were only a short distance away. Alan held me in an iron grip. It would be very easy for him to drag me to the edge and throw me over.

Instead, to my astonishment, he suddenly shoved me away from him, so hard that I slipped on the wet ground and fell to my knees.

'Walt,' he said aloud. Then he repeated it, this time as a yell. 'Walt!'

He turned away from me and began to run, in the direction of Farroday's cottage.

Until now, I had expected Alan to relive the scenes between himself and Emily. I had forgotten altogether the part played in the past by that other lighthouse keeper, Walt. Now I remembered the vicious fight that had taken place between those two men. This was the scene that Alan was running now to reenact, except that Walt was no longer in that cottage, Farroday was, and in a moment an unsuspecting Farroday was going to be attacked by Alan, crazed out of his mind.

I had to stop Alan. Both men were strong, but Alan was driven by the demons of his past. There was no telling what he might do before he could be made to realize who it was he was fighting.

Before I could even get to my feet, though, I heard another voice, coming from the darkness behind me.

'Karen,' it called.

My heart skipped a beat. I remembered the night that Alan and I had pursued a ghostly voice over the cliffs. I turned and saw a shadow moving among the shadows, separating itself from them to come toward me.

10

I had a moment of relief when I saw that it was Mrs. Denver approaching. Her dark slicker had blended with the night, making her almost invisible until she was close.

'Listen,' I told her urgently. 'Alan's gone off after Walt. There's no telling what will happen when he gets to Farroday's cottage. We've got to stop him.'

I started to get up but I had turned my ankle and a flash of pain shot up from it. 'I've hurt my foot,' I said, rubbing it gingerly. 'You go ahead. I'll hobble along as best I can.'

She did not move, however. I had been examining my ankle. Now for the first time I really looked at her. When I did, I got a shock. She was holding a gun, aimed directly at me.

'What on earth is that for?' I said.

She looked mad. Close on I could see

that her eyes were gleaming and wide. Her lips curled in a vicious snarl. 'You little fool,' she said in a voice that dripped venom.

My mind was racing. She was beyond herself, lost in some world of anger and resentment toward me. I had to find some way to get past the barrier of that resentment. I used the one thing I thought would distract her from whatever she intended with the gun.

'Alan,' I said, speaking firmly and clearly. 'Never mind about me. You've got to stop him before he does another wrong.'

'I warned you that you were playing with fire,' she said, ignoring my plea. 'I tried to convince you to go away, for Alan's sake, for your own sake. Well, now you'll have to pay the consequences. Just like that little fool Emily.'

I could say nothing. It was grotesque, kneeling in the cold and the rain while she stood over me, gun in hand, talking with a chilling calm.

I had never been so frightened before. Ghosts and strange voices were eerie but they did not give the sense of personal threat that I was feeling just now. Her hatred for me was like a living thing reaching out across the brief distance that separated us, curling its icy fingers about me. For the first time in my life I knew that I was in the very presence of death.

'She was crazy, Emily was,' she said. 'Did the dear Doctor Kramer tell you that? Mad as a hatter, she was. Oh, she pretended to be all right. When I asked her about it, she said she had been treated and she was just fine.'

She threw back her head and laughed. The hood of her raincoat fell loose and the rain instantly made a shambles of her hair, so that she looked like nothing so much as one of Macbeth's witches.

'Crazy as a loon. And she tried to take my place in Alan's life. *My place*. The years I had lived here, alone, miserable. I gave my life to this damned Point. To my husband, because he wouldn't go away even when I begged him. And then to my son, because he'd grown up here and loved it, he said it was in his blood.

'Year after year, enduring the isolation,

and the starkness and the danger, fighting the elements, gradually winning some peace over them. And then, just when everything looked all right, just when I was finally beginning to feel happy here, she came to take my place. I wanted to kill her from the first moment I set eyes on her. I could think of nothing but how much I'd love to wring her neck.'

She said this last with such vehemence that I did not for a moment think she was exaggerating. I shuddered, thinking not only of the hatred she had felt for Emily, but realizing as well that she must have felt the same — perhaps even worse — when she had first seen me. And I had hoped we could become friends!

'I tried to scare her away. I wouldn't have harmed her if she had gone. What did I care what happened to her? It was Alan I cared about. Alan and my own peace of mind. And my rights. I had rights, too. I'd earned them. I'd bought them with my life. Forty years of enduring here. And she had taken everything away in one night.

'Well, I meant to get it back. She was

scared to death here, scared of her own shadow, and I played on that. I talked about ghosts, as if they were real. When I knew she was alone, I would come and tap on the window and beckon her outside.'

'That was you,' I said, realizing how she had tried the same tactics with me. 'And you locked me in the lighthouse, didn't you? And called to Alan in the night?'

She laughed, a weird sound that lifted on the wind and rushed along the cliffs. 'Yes. I thought I could scare you away. You little fool, you should have gone. It would have saved your life.'

She brandished the gun in a threatening manner. My mind raced frantically, searching for something to say. 'Emily didn't go either, did she?' I said, grasping at straws.

It brought her back to her narrative. She seemed to need for me to understand, and I watched and listened raptly, for all the world as if I did not know that at any moment now she was going to try to kill me.

'No, she didn't go. She just got crazier.

And she got Walt to listen to her. I hadn't counted on him, but that worked out just fine, too. He knew she was crazy. He didn't care. It didn't affect what he wanted from her. He didn't mind patting her hand while she unburdened herself to him. He encouraged her fantasies. And then came that night.'

She paused for a long time. Her eyes seemed to look through me rather than at me, and I knew she was really looking into the past, seeing that night recreated as if upon a stage.

'That night,' she said, dropping her voice so low that I actually had to strain to hear everything, 'Alan came to me in a frenzy. I encouraged it. I told him all sorts of things about her, I said anything I could think of to anger him further. And he was in a state of mind to believe everything I told him.

'Finally, he could bear no more. He rushed from the house. I saw that he had taken the road. I grabbed my coat and came by the cliff path. I know every rock along the way. I could run it blindfolded. I ran like a demon. I wasn't afraid. Those cliffs long ago lost any power to frighten me.

'I was here long before he was. I let myself into the house and I found Emily in her room, the one she'd reserved for her own personal use. She was out of her head. She had put on her wedding dress and was sitting by the window, just smiling and looking out. She said someone was coming for her.

'I talked to her of the ghosts. By then I knew how to play on her mind, on her fears. It was as easy as pie. I had her scared out of her wits again in a matter of minutes, jumping every time the floorboards creaked.

'She began to cry and shake. She begged me not to leave her. She pleaded for me to make the ghosts go away.

''There's only one way to free yourself of these awful spirits,' I told her. 'They've claimed you for one of their own. They will haunt you for as long as you live.''

I gasped aloud as the implication became clear to me. 'You drove her to the cliffs.'

'She was crazy. She'd have done it

sooner or later anyway. I just convinced her it was the right time. I took her outside. I showed her the cliffs. I told her that it would take one step, just one step beyond that rock there, and she would be at peace, free of Alan, free of the Point, free of the ghosts that tormented her.

'I told her not to walk, not to think about it, just to run, until there was no ground left to run upon.

'Alan came then. He saw her and tried to stop her, but he fell, and she went over, and it was all done. I was so overjoyed when I discovered that he couldn't remember any of it. Emily was gone. Alan knew nothing of her existence. It was as if none of it had ever happened, as if the entire business had been erased from the book of time.'

She paused, and said in a different voice, 'Until you came.'

I had finally heard the story I had been trying to learn, the entire, true story — too late to help Alan, or me.

'Now,' she said, 'I have it all to do over again. I saved my son from one foolish marriage only to see him make the same mistake again. You must have been mad to think I would let you get away with it. Did you really think I would just step aside, throw away all my years of sacrifice and work, so that you could be happy?'

'And what of Alan's happiness?' I asked, my voice breaking at the end. 'Don't you care about his happiness either?'

'Alan?' She spat the word at me. 'Alan was happy before you came, happy with me. He's always been happy with me. It's only when someone tries to take my place that he's unhappy. He was miserable with her, any fool could see that. He would have killed her if I hadn't driven her to kill herself.'

'I can't believe that's true,' I said. 'No matter how angry you made him he would never have done that. You're only trying to absolve your own guilt.'

She seemed not to have heard me at all. 'And he's been unhappy with you,' she said. 'I've tried to help. I've tried to frighten you away too. I've begged you to go, but you wouldn't. Now I shall have to deal with you. Now you shall have to die.'

The gun was pointing at my head. I knew that I was seconds away from death. I tried desperately to think of something to say.

'You can't just murder me, don't you see? They'll know. You can't explain away a bullet wound very easily.'

'Oh, I have it all thought out.' She smiled as if she were proud of her cleverness and expected me to be proud of her too. Mingled with my fear was a sense of pity for her. I knew what Emily had suffered here.

This woman had suffered it too, for forty years. Under the strain of loneliness, perhaps in the company of a husband who did not love or understand her, her mind had given out too — not in a dramatic way, as Emily's had done, but slowly rotting from within, leaving her twisted and selfish. All those years she had lived virtually by herself. Now she could see no alternative to living for herself.

'No one will be surprised to learn that you're a little mad too,' she said. 'They'll probably expect it. After all, Alan picked

245

you as nearly a duplicate of Emily. I've already let it be known that you're strange. People already know that you've been seeing and hearing things just as she used to do.'

I thought of Mrs. Scruggs, who had suddenly taken a cool attitude toward me. I had no doubt that her ears had been filled with peculiar stories. The woman in town, too. A few whispered words of poison had been enough to plant the seeds of suspicion.

'Better yet, you've given me the ultimate proof,' she said, chuckling. 'There you are, all dressed up in Emily's wedding gown. I'll say you thought Emily's spirit had taken over your body, that you were possessed.'

With mounting horror I saw how I had played into her hands. To an outsider there would seem to be no other explanation for my wearing this tattered gown. She would have no difficulty at all explaining away the fact that I too, as Emily had done, had thrown myself from the cliffs.

There was one flaw in her scheme,

246

however. 'I'll never jump,' I said. 'You can't drive me to that the way you did that poor frightened girl you murdered.'

After a moment of silence, she sighed. 'But it won't make that much difference. I can just as well use the gun. It's Alan's, you see. I'll say that he shot you. It will be like it was before. He'll blot it all out of his mind and my story will be the one everyone will accept.'

'But you can't do that to him,' I cried. 'Alan will be a murderer. They'll send him to the chair.'

'I think not. Think of how it will look. His mental state is well known. He came along the path at night, in a storm. He saw what he thought was the ghost of his dead wife. You're wearing her gown, you have your hair pulled back the way she always wore hers. Who would ever blame him for reacting violently?'

I could see that she was right. Chances were, she would be able to get away with her awful scheme. I had myself created the perfect situation for her.

'You'll never get away with it,' I said. 'No one will believe those stories again.'

I was speaking in desperation, stalling for time. I felt out with my hand, hunting for some sort of weapon, a stone perhaps, but I found nothing. When I brought my hand back to my foot, I had one spark of hope.

'What if Alan has gotten his memory back?' I slipped one of my shoes off. It was a sodden mess now, but the feel of it in my hand gave me at least a slim chance.

'I'm not worried about Alan. If worse comes to worst, he'll do what I tell him. But we've talked long enough. I want to be done with this.'

She had let the gun aim downward slightly while she talked. Now, her purpose horribly clear, she lifted it again.

I threw the shoe with all the strength I could muster. It struck the gun and knocked it from her hand. It clattered to the ground somewhere behind her, in the darkness.

At the same moment, I scrambled to my feet. My ankle gave a stab of pain, but it held me up.

'Blast you,' she cried, stooping down to

look for the gun.

I turned and began to run, limping along frantically. I had no clear-cut plan. My only hope was that I might find a place among the rocks to hide from her until Alan came back. She would never dare to harm me in his presence, whatever she thought in her warped mind.

'Stop,' she cried, suddenly realizing that I was trying to escape. She sprang to her feet, racing after me.

I had the advantage of youth, but with my bad ankle I was no match for her.

In a moment she was upon me. She had a manic strength. Her face, so close to mine, was awful, twisted into a grotesque mask of hatred.

We fought savagely. I was fighting for my life, and desperation gave me a strength I had never possessed before, but she was hard and wiry. She had lived a rough life on these cliffs and she was as strong as a man.

With a sob in my throat, I realized she was edging me backward, toward the cliff's edge. I tried to break free of her grip but I could not. Step by step we were inching closer to the rim. The elements seemed to conspire to help her. I felt as if the wind were pushing me along, as if the ground were tilting toward that jagged point where the earth ended. The waves themselves seemed to shriek my name.

'Don't, in the name of God,' I gasped. She had one hand at my throat and I was growing weaker by the moment. I could see over the edge now, we were so close to it. Phosphorous gleamed on the lashing waves below, as if they were trimmed in lace.

'Karen.'

At first I thought it was only a trick of the wind, but this was no fantasy. It was Alan, not a ghost from my terrified imagination.

I managed to wrench away the hand that clasped my throat. 'Alan,' I screamed. 'Alan, here, hurry!'

'Karen?' he sounded far away — too far away.

I tried with the last of my strength to break free, but my foot slipped and I fell. My head struck hard against a rock. The world swooped and spun. I fought to cling to consciousness. Lights flashed before my eyes.

Strong hands seized my shoulders and I was being dragged over the hard ground. Even in my dazed state I knew where I was being dragged.

'Karen? Mother? What's going on?' He was closer.

The hands released their grip on me. I fell to the ground again, unable to hold myself up. For a moment there were only the sounds of the night. Then, suddenly, a horrible scream rent the air.

I pushed myself up to a sitting position. I saw Alan running hard toward me, but there was no sign of his mother. I turned my head. The edge of the cliff was inches away and beyond it only sky and sea, and far away over the water, the beam from the lighthouse, moving like an accusing finger.

Then I was in Alan's arms, sobbing against his chest. Behind him I saw Farroday, standing grimly still.

'Are you all right?' Alan asked me after a moment. I managed to nod my head.

'Your mother . . . ' I began, but I couldn't finish.

'She tried to kill you, didn't she?' His face, so near my own, was pale and drawn with grief.

I nodded again, biting my lip to try to hold back my sobs.

'She killed Emily, too.'

That was all he said just then, and I was still too shaken to speak. I let my head fall against his chest once more, but even though I was crying, I knew that everything was going to be all right. My desperate scheme had worked.

Alan remembered.

★ ★ ★

I've never known just what did happen that night. I don't know whether, in springing away from me in the hope that Alan hadn't seen what she was trying to do, his mother had simply lost her balance and fallen over the edge. Or whether, knowing that Alan had seen her and her desperate charade was doomed, she had followed Emily's tragic example.

I thought perhaps Alan knew the truth, that he had seen, but he never offered to speak of it and I never asked.

I did learn that he had burst into Farroday's cottage, expecting to find a man named Walt. I shudder to think what might have happened if Farroday had been the sort to panic, but he had not. He had been able to calm Alan and with calm, Alan's memory had come back.

'It didn't come back all at once,' he explained to me later. 'It was sort of bits and pieces, until finally there were enough pieces to put the picture back together again. When I did, I came looking for you right off.'

I avoided making much of what had happened, but we both knew I had been seconds away from death and that only his arrival on the scene had saved me.

As for the rest, he remembered everything now. 'It's as if a curtain were lifted. A moment before everything was out of sight and now suddenly there it all was, before my eyes. I was trying to face up to the fact of my mother's domination. I could understand the reasons for her possessiveness and I was trying to break away from it as easily as possible.

'I think I saw Emily as a means of establishing my independence, and later, that was a part of my guilt. If I had really loved her, I'd have gone away with her, or tried harder to understand — anything but just ignored her fear and unhappiness.'

'Whatever your guilt, you've suffered enough. No doubt you were in part to blame, but I truly doubt if you could have made things come out differently. Emily's mind was already damaged and your mother was determined to take advantage of that.'

He took my hand in his. 'Thank God there's nothing weak about you.' He paused before adding, 'You know, it may be that the similarities in appearance influenced my first impression of you. I don't know that much about psychology. But I know that I fell in love with you, not with some ghost from the past. I've grown more deeply in love with you with every passing day.'

He kissed me and all the fears of the

past faded away, never to return. Alan was free of his ghosts now, free to love me as I loved him, with all, not just half of his heart and mind.

In the distance I heard the murmur of the waves, but their tone now was approving, not threatening.

THE END

We do hope that you have enjoyed reading this large print book.

Did you know that all of our titles are available for purchase?

We publish a wide range of high quality large print books including:
Romances, Mysteries, Classics
General Fiction
Non Fiction and Westerns

Special interest titles available in large print are:
The Little Oxford Dictionary
Music Book, Song Book
Hymn Book, Service Book

Also available from us courtesy of Oxford University Press:
Young Readers' Dictionary
(large print edition)
Young Readers' Thesaurus
(large print edition)

For further information or a free brochure, please contact us at:
Ulverscroft Large Print Books Ltd.,
The Green, Bradgate Road, Anstey,
Leicester, LE7 7FU, England.
Tel: (00 44) 0116 236 4325
Fax: (00 44) 0116 234 0205

Other titles in the
Linford Mystery Library:

ZONE ZERO

John Robb

Western powers plan to explode a hydrogen bomb in a remote area of Southern Algeria — code named Zone Zero. The zone has to be evacuated. Fort Ney is the smallest Foreign Legion outpost in the zone, commanded by a young lieutenant. Here, too, is the English legionnaire, tortured by previous cowardice, as well as a little Greek who has within him the spark of greatness. It has always been a peaceful place — until the twelve travellers arrive. Now the outwitted garrison faces the uttermost limit of horror . . .

THE WEIRD SHADOW OVER MORECAMBE

Edmund Glasby

Professor Mandrake Smith would be unrecognisable to his former colleagues now: the shambling, drink-addled erstwhile Professor of Anthropology at Oxford is now barely surviving in Morecambe. He has many things to forget, although some don't want to forget him. Plagued by nightmares from his past, both in Oxford and Papua New Guinea, he finds himself drafted by the enigmatic Mr. Thorn, whom he grudgingly assists in trying to stop the downward spiral into darkness and insanity that awaits Morecambe — and the entire world . . .